Twelfth Night Proposal

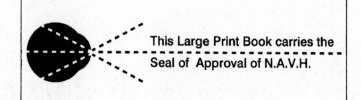

Twelfth Night Proposal

Karen Rose Smith

Thorndike Press • Waterville, Maine

Published in 2006 by arrangement with Harlequin Books S.A.

Thorndike Press® Large Print Romance.

The tree indicium is a trademark of Thorndike Press.

The text of this Large Print edition is unabridged.
Other aspects of the book may vary from the original edition.

Set in 16 pt. Plantin by Myrna S. Raven.

Printed in the United States on permanent paper.

Library of Congress Cataloging-in-Publication Data

Smith, Karen Rose.
    Twelfth night proposal / Karen Rose Smith.
        p. cm. — (Shakespeare in love)
    (Thorndike Press large print romance)
    ISBN 0-7862-8636-9 (lg. print : hc : alk. paper)
    1. Nannies — Fiction.   2. Fathers and daughters —
Fiction.   3. Large type books.   I. Title.   II. Series:
Thorndike Press large print romance series.   III. Series.
PS3569.M5375537T86 2006
    813′.54—dc22   2006006967

To Jeanne Smith — Appreciation for the Bard was one of our first connections. Thanks for your friendship and support. With thanks to Stella Bagwell, my Texas Gulf authority.

Cast of Characters

Leo Montgomery (Lead Character) — This angst-ridden dad thought he'd lost the only love of his life. Until he hired a nanny for his daughter and found her taking up residence in his home . . . and heart.

Verity Sumpter (Lead Character) — Ever since her twin brother's death, this plain Jane had kept her true self hidden behind shapeless clothes and wire-rimmed glasses. But the widower and his adorable daughter suddenly had her wanting to shed her drab attire and embrace life. . . .

Heather Montgomery (Supporting Character) — This bubbly three-year-old longed for a mother. And she'd found the perfect candidate in her new nanny. But how could she convince her stubborn dad that sometimes children really do know best?

Prologue

Montgomery Boat Company
Avon Lake, Texas

Glancing at the TV in his office, Leo Montgomery saw paradise. Well, a spot that was *supposed* to be paradise. There was a lake and grass and trees and a guy dressed in a tuxedo. But it wasn't the guy who captured Leo's attention.

There was a woman. The perfect fantasy woman.

Leo glimpsed her face for a moment — maybe half a moment — less time than it took to take a breath. He caught the sparkling, huge brown eyes. Then she was turning . . . away from him. When she turned, his palms tingled to touch her long, curly brown hair with its red highlights reflecting the sun. The dress she wore was some wispy material. It was short and bared most of her back, the fabric molding to her long legs as she walked away from the camera and away from him. She handed the guy in the tuxedo a can of soda. Large red letters proclaimed its name

— ZING. Leo's gaze was still on the woman's back and those curls. When she lifted a parasol, tilted it over her shoulder and walked away, the letters on the parasol spelled ZING, The Fantasy Soda. As the jingle for ZING filled the airwaves, she disappeared into the trees.

To Leo's amazement, he found himself aroused . . . stirred in a way he hadn't been stirred for a very long time. Since well before Carolyn's death two years ago, for sure.

Giving himself a mental shake, willing his libido to calm down, Leo flicked off the TV with the remote. That fantasy woman on the screen was just that — a fantasy. He knew better than most men that fantasies don't become reality. On the other hand, however, maybe he should think about getting involved with someone from his country club. As his sister, Jolene, told him often, Heather needed a mother. His daughter needed more than the nanny-housekeeper Jolene had just hired.

Heather needed a mother, and *he* didn't want to sleep alone for the rest of his life.

Although the cursor on the computer screen blinked before him, Leo couldn't forget the fantasy woman's mass of reddish-brown curls, those long legs, that bare back.

He couldn't remember a feature on the model's face, but he supposed that was the whole idea — to charge a man's fantasy. Nevertheless, Leo wasn't the type of man to dwell on fantasies when reality was sitting right in front of him.

He checked the information on the computer with the boatyard orders on his desk. The dream woman forgotten, work filled his head. That's the way he wanted it for now. Jolene's advice might be sound, but he wasn't ready for it. He wasn't ready for involvement or commitment.

That's just the way it was.

Chapter One

"Montgomery here," Leo said as he flipped open his silver cell phone and stepped away from the boat trailer into the hot December sun.

"This is Verity. Heather's nanny."

The fact that he had to be reminded of her job position spoke of how little he'd paid attention to the new nanny. Maybe that was because he expected her to come and go as the rest had. Maybe it was because of her glasses, tied-back hair and oversize T-shirts. For almost a month she'd moved around like a ghost in his house, seemingly quite capable, as Jolene had predicted she would be, yet definitely always in the background.

Now he was on the alert because this call most probably concerned his daughter. "Verity, what is it?"

"It's Heather. I didn't want to bother you, but I thought you should know that she fell against the coffee table in the great room and cut her forehead."

Leo's heart pounded and he felt panic grip him. "Is she all right? Did you take her to the emergency room?"

"I applied pressure and used a butterfly bandage, but you might want to have her checked. Just tell me what you'd like me to do."

Merely three, with her light-brown, wavy hair and her blue, blue eyes, all Heather had to do was look at him and his heart melted. The thought of her hurt —

"I'll be right there. Fifteen minutes tops. Is she crying? Is she upset?"

Verity's voice was helpfully patient. "She's sitting in my lap, sucking her thumb with her head on my shoulder."

"I'll be there as soon as I tell my foreman where I'm going. Keep her calm and call me if you see any change."

"Yes, Mr. Montgomery."

Leo headed for the production plant.

Fifteen minutes later he arrived at his house in a select section of Avon Lake, Texas, where the houses in his development were quietly luxurious. His ranch house sat back from the curb with a curved drive leading to it. He left the car in the driveway and hurried to the front door.

Usually when he came home, he was filled with the same sense of well-being he felt at the boatyard. Today dread clouded his thoughts as it had when he'd learned about Carolyn's brain tumor. What if Heather had seriously injured herself? What if she had a concussion?

His boots sounded on the ceramic tile floor in the entrance foyer as he headed straight ahead for the great room. The fireplace, cathedral ceiling and skylights made it his favorite room in the house. He barely noticed any of that now as he hurried to the denim sofa where Verity was seated with Heather. His daughter was dressed in red overalls with a little white sweater underneath. Her cheeks were pink and tear-stained, and her eyes were wide, as she kept her head on Verity's shoulder and stared up at him.

"Hello, baby," he said as he went to take her into his arms. To his surprise she hung on to Verity.

Verity whispered to her, "Go with Daddy."

But Heather shook her head, held on even tighter and mumbled around her thumb, "I wanna stay wif you."

Leo felt a stab to his heart.

With understanding eyes, Verity looked up at him, and Leo saw her, *really* saw her, for the first time since she'd been hired. There was a quiet equanimity about her that had calmed him from the first moment he'd met her. She was young — twenty-two. Her major in college had been early childhood education, and in the short time she'd been with him, she handled Heather as if she knew exactly what she was doing. He had a feeling that had more to do with natural ability than any schooling. Her blue wire-rim glasses had always distracted him from looking at her eyes before now. They were a beautiful brown, the color of teak. Her hair, tied back in a low ponytail, looked silky and soft. Her face was a classic oval, and her nose turned up just a bit at the tip. Although here on the Gulf most residents were suntanned, he noticed Verity's skin was creamy white.

"She's still upset," Verity said.

"Instead of the E.R., we'll take her to the pediatrician. I called him on the drive here. He said to bring her right in."

With utmost gentleness, Verity stroked Heather's hair. "Do you want me to go along?"

"I don't think I can pry her away from you," he responded wryly, realizing how that bothered him. Apparently, Heather had connected with this nanny. He was grateful for that, yet —

"Let's go," he directed gruffly, and

would have turned to leave, but then he realized he'd been doing everything in a hurry lately. He'd also been working long hours. How many nights had he put Heather to bed since Verity had arrived and started caring for her?

Apparently not enough.

"Let's go with Daddy," Verity murmured to the little girl.

Leo looked at Verity again and found himself thinking how pretty she was, even though she was sloppily dressed. He found himself liking the sound of her voice. He found himself . . . getting stirred up in a way a man shouldn't around a nanny.

Their gazes connected and, in a flash, he saw the same man-woman awareness in her eyes that he was feeling. Then she glanced away, and he was glad. He certainly didn't want to delve further into that.

In his SUV, driving toward the doctor's office, an awkward silence surrounded them.

Leo headed north on Lonestar Way, Avon Lake's main thoroughfare, leading toward the college side of town. The college housed about 10,000 students, and the town itself had a growing population of more than 7,000 now. But Leo knew Avon

Lake would always keep that small-town flavor. At least, he hoped it would.

Heather's pediatrician was located in one of the old houses near the college. Leo knew Verity took a course at the campus once a week, though he didn't know much else about her, except what she'd given on her résumé. She'd attended college at the University of Texas and had been born and bred in Galveston.

Maybe because of his reaction to her for those few moments, maybe because her silence made him wonder what she was thinking, he asked her, "What course are you taking this semester?"

As she shifted in her seat, he felt her gaze fall upon him. "I'm not taking a class officially. When I accepted the position with you in November, I was too late to register for the term. But I'm auditing a class on children's play techniques."

"You're working on your master's?"

"Yes, I hope to. I have an advisor now. I'll be meeting with him soon to choose courses for next term."

"It's hard to believe Christmas is less than a month away. Did you have an enjoyable Thanksgiving?"

They hadn't talked since then, and Leo didn't even know where she'd gone. She'd left early in the morning and come back late that evening after he and Heather had returned from dinner at Jolene's.

Quiet for a few moments, Verity finally answered, "It was fine."

Casting a sideways glance at her, his interest was piqued, maybe because of everything she wasn't saying. "Did you spend it with family?"

"No. I went to Freeport for the day."

"And met friends?"

Again, that little silence, and then she shook her head. "No, I had dinner, then I drove to the beach for a while."

Now he was even more intrigued. Didn't she have family? Why would she spend the holiday alone? If he asked those questions, he'd become more involved than he wanted to be.

Heather suddenly called from the back in her superfast baby voice. "Vewitee. Vewitee. I wanna feed duckee and go for ice cweam."

Verity gave her full attention to Heather as she turned. "Not today, honey. We have to go to the doctor's so he can look at your head."

"No doctor. I wanna feed duckees."

Peering into the rearview mirror to see his daughter, Leo caught sight of her lower

18

lip pouting out. He hated to see her cry. "What if we go feed the ducks after the doctor looks at your head?"

After thinking about that for a few moments, she returned, "Ice cweam, too?"

"It's going to be close to supper. Maybe we could stop at the Wagon Wheel and get that chicken you like so much. They have ice cream for dessert."

"Chicken and ice cweam!" Heather said gleefully.

Verity laughed, a pure, free sound that entranced Leo, as she commented, "Ducks, chicken and ice cream all in one day. She's going to hold you to every one of those."

"Like an elephant never forgets?" he asked with a chuckle.

"Something like that. I can't believe how her vocabulary is growing, just in the few weeks I've been here. Each day she's becoming more coordinated, too. I've seen it before, of course, with the children I've worked with, but just caring for one child, and seeing her change almost daily, is absolutely amazing."

"I know Jolene probably mentioned it, but I don't remember how you heard about the position with me," he prompted.

"I have a friend in the career counseling office at UT. She knew I was looking for a

19

change, called me and told me about it."

"A change from what you were doing or where you were living?"

"Both."

That concise word was the end of the conversation unless Leo wanted to pursue it. He didn't.

Sitting beside Verity, smelling the floral scent of her shampoo or lotion, very much liking the sound of her laughter, he felt as if he were awakening from a long sleep. It was disconcerting. He'd gotten used to his life, and although Jolene often told him he was in a rut, ruts were damned comfortable.

Activities in the town of Avon Lake often revolved around the small lake. After Leo unfastened Heather from her car seat and lifted her to the ground, she took Verity's hand and ran toward the black and gray ducks on the grassy shoreline.

In a few quick strides, Leo caught up to them, the bag of crackers he'd bought at a convenience store in his hand. "Wait a minute. You forgot something. You can't feed them if you don't have the food."

When Heather stopped short, let go of Verity's hand and ran back to him, he crouched down. "Do you want me to open the bag or do you want to try it?"

"*Me* try."

He handed it to her. But after jabs and pulls and a few squishes, she shook her head, curling tendrils along her cheek bobbing all over the place. "Can't do it. You open, please."

Leo knew his daughter's face was as close to an angel's as he'd ever see. Taking the bag between his two large hands, he pulled and a corner popped open. "There you go. Break up each one so they have lots of little pieces."

After Heather nodded vigorously, she took the bag and ran for the lake.

"Wait," he and Verity called at the same time and ran after her.

As he caught one of Heather's hands, Verity held her elbow. "Don't spill the crackers," she warned with a smile.

The sun's brilliance was fading into long shadows, though the air was warm and the day was still above 70. Standing by a tall pecan tree, Leo watched Verity as she and Heather sat on the grass and two ducks waddled closer. Heather crushed a cracker in her hand and opened her little fingers, waving her arm in the air. The crumbs blew this way and that. One of the ducks quacked and ran after a piece and she laughed like only a three-year-old could.

The doctor's exam had gone smoothly and quickly, mostly thanks to Verity. She seemed to be able to read his daughter's mind . . . seemed to know what to say to coax her into acquiescence. He didn't have that knack. He was learning negotiation was the highest skill a parent could master.

As he watched his daughter, he felt removed and didn't like it. After taking a few steps closer, he sat with Verity and Heather.

Heather offered him the bag. "You feed duckees, too."

How long had it been since he'd taken time to do just that? Taking one of the crackers from the bag, he broke it into a few pieces and tossed them so Heather could watch the ducks waddle after them.

"I should bring her here more often," he decided reflectively.

"You could use it as a treat so it doesn't become old hat."

Staring into Verity's brown eyes, feeling that stirring again, he said, "You're very good with her."

"Thank you. I've been waiting for some kind of sign from you —" She stopped and looked embarrassed.

"Sign?"

"Yes. To know if I'm doing a good job . . . to know if I'm doing what you want me to do with Heather. She's a wonderful little girl and I love being with her. But you're her parent, and I want to make sure she's learning what *you* want her to learn."

What *he* wanted her to learn.

He knew Verity wasn't talking about colors and numbers. "Jolene hired you and gave you a seal of approval, so I guess I thought that was enough. As she probably told you, I've tried nannies before. After two days, I know whether they're going to last or not . . . whether they fit with Heather or not. I fired one because she just wanted to watch TV and read all day and left Heather on her own. Another quit because she said she didn't have enough free time. You might decide that's true for you, too."

"I don't need much free time."

Curious, he asked, "Why not?"

"I'm new in town. I really don't know anyone. So when I'm free, I study for the course I'm auditing, read or knit. I'm not very exciting," she admitted, her cheeks pinkening a little.

The blush looked good on her. In fact, he was having trouble unlocking his gaze from hers. "You'll have friends once you start taking more courses. That is, if you stay."

"I'm exactly where I want to be right now," she murmured softly, and he felt himself almost leaning toward her. He imagined she had slightly leaned toward him. The urge to reach out and run his thumb along her cheek was so strong he balled his hand into a fist. He didn't know what was going on today, but he didn't like it.

After he picked up the bag of crackers, he motioned to Heather. "Come on, let's feed more ducks. Those over there didn't get any yet."

He was twelve years older than this young woman who'd begun to fascinate him. He'd never given a glance to younger women before. Not only was she younger, but he saw vulnerability and innocence in those eyes. He could be wrong, but he doubted it. No matter what her life story, it was safest for him to keep his distance.

That was exactly what he was going to do.

Each stroke of Verity Sumpter's hairbrush through her hair was meant to be monotonous and soothing, but it wasn't. All too easily she could imagine Mr. Montgomery's hands stroking her hair. The

24

thoughts were making her hot, bothered and agitated. From the moment she'd set eyes on Leo Montgomery her heart had tripped a little. If she had to admit it, her heart had tripped a lot. Today was the first he'd noticed her . . . *really* noticed her.

He'd probably have noticed her from day one if she'd applied makeup, highlighted her hair, spent the time on spiral curls and dolled herself up, as the casting agent had for that commercial she'd made.

That commercial.

Her twin brother, Sean, had encouraged her to do it and teased her saying, maybe if she did, she'd forget her tomboy days forever. Dear Sean.

When tears came to her eyes, she let them well up this time as she pulled her hair into a ponytail. He'd been gone for eleven months now, and the missing still overwhelmed her sometimes. She and Sean had been as close as any twins could have been. They'd shared secrets and jokes and sports and even attended the same college. He'd screened her dates and she'd always looked over the girls he'd brought home.

When a casting agent had approached her in the library on campus, he'd explained he was looking for college girls to make a series of commercials for a new

25

soda — the company was targeting the college crowd. Verity hadn't given much thought to the idea until Sean had heard about it. He'd teased, cajoled and coaxed, insisting the experience would be good for her.

Her straight-as-a-ruler hair had become a mass of curls. She'd traded her glasses for contact lenses, and makeup had made her eyes look huge and her lips much fuller. No one knew if the commercial would ever make it to the TV screen, and she hadn't heard anything from the company other than receiving her payment for the hours she'd worked as a model.

After the shoot, Verity had decided curling her hair for an hour or more, applying makeup and dressing up was all simply too much trouble. The red highlights washed out of her hair, and eventually the curls straightened into looser waves and were caught up in a practical ponytail once more. When one of the soft contact lenses had torn, she'd gone back to using her glasses.

Then, last January, Sean had the skiing accident. When he'd died, her life had fallen apart. She'd gone through the motions to earn her diploma —

Noise in the hall startled Verity. Her

bedroom, sitting area and bathroom were located at the opposite end of the house from the master suite and Heather's bedroom, along with another guest bedroom. Mr. Montgomery took over Heather's care on the rare nights he was home and, after he'd put Heather to bed, she usually didn't hear another sound.

Now, however, she heard little feet slapping on the hardwood floor, Leo's deep baritone calling, "Heather, you come back here," and the little girl's giggles as she came closer to Verity's door.

Verity had crossed into the sitting area when the door burst open and Heather ran through the room, naked, the ends of her hair wet, soapsuds still on her shoulders. The bump on her head hadn't slowed her down one iota.

Halfway across Verity's sitting room, Leo stopped. "I shouldn't have come in here without knocking."

Verity laughed. "I think Heather took care of announcing you."

Leo shook his head. "I'll collect her if she doesn't squiggle out of my arms again. She is so slippery when she's wet —"

"And she hates to stand still while you dry her off. I know."

Her gaze collided with his, and there was

that shakingly fascinating awareness again.

Breaking eye contact, he said, "Since I consider your room to be off-limits to me, do you want me to get her or do you want to do it?"

"I don't mind if you do," Verity murmured as she continued to stare at him. Leo was still wearing the black polo shirt and khakis he'd had on that afternoon. He was tanned, and his arm muscles were obvious under the shirtsleeves. His stomach was flat and she suspected hard. His hips were slim.

When he turned, she chastised herself for liking every bit of his backside, too. She couldn't be attracted to her employer. Besides the fact that she was tired of men letting her down, she was much younger than Leo Montgomery. She'd seen the picture of Heather's mother in the little girl's room. Carolyn Montgomery had looked poised with her perfect makeup and blond pageboy. She was absolutely beautiful. Verity imagined any woman would have trouble living up to that. Jolene Connehy, Mr. Montgomery's sister, had told her honestly that he wasn't over his wife's death, even though it had been two years. Verity could understand that. She knew she'd never get over losing Sean.

Leo stepped into Verity's bedroom, and the very fact that he was so near her double bed disconcerted her. Maybe because ever since this afternoon pictures had been swimming in her head — pictures of Leo kissing her, pictures of her kissing him back.

His gaze had gone to the bed, too, with its white chenille spread, its maple bookcase headboard, where she'd lined up some of her favorite reads. But her mind wasn't on her books as she said in almost a whisper, "She likes to play hide-and-seek under the bed."

With a shake of his head, as if he couldn't believe he was doing this, he got down on his knees and lifted the edge of the spread. His voice was filled with affectionate frustration as he called, "Hey, you. You've got to get out from under there and put on some pajamas."

"I don't wanna go nighty-night. Wanna play with Vewitee."

Without hesitation Verity got down on the floor beside Leo. Her shoulder brushed his as she peered under the bed at her little charge. The touch of her shirt against his sent a jolt of adrenaline rushing through her. "If you come out and put on your pj's, I'll read you a story."

"That's bribery," Leo murmured very close to her ear, his breath warm on her cheek. Verity shivered.

"Would you rather kneel here and cajole for the next half hour?" she asked him, half joking, half serious.

"I'm too big to fit under the bed, and cajoling isn't my style."

"That leaves bribery," she decided, unable to suppress a grin.

His face was so very close to hers as they focused on Heather. When he turned his head to her, mere inches separated their lips. Leo's scent was pure male, and his light-brown hair fell over his brow in a rakish way. But it was the gleam of raw hunger in his eyes that kept her immobilized.

Suddenly he cleared his throat, bent lower, and extended his arm under the bed. "Come on, you little hooligan. Verity will read you a story. But don't think this is going to happen again. Next time I won't let you out of the bathroom until you have your pj's on."

Quickly recovering from whatever had overcome her when she'd been so close to Leo, Verity teased, "You really shouldn't tell her your strategy."

"Good advice," he admitted as Heather

started wriggling toward them from under the bed.

"I'll go get her pajamas. Try to keep her from hiding anyplace else until I get back."

Verity laughed. "She likes me to brush her hair. I'll do that."

Less than five minutes later, Leo had returned with Heather's pajamas and Verity had helped him get her into them. She watched him as he fastened two small buttons at the three-year-old's neck, and his fingers fumbled with them. He was such a big man, but he was gentle with his daughter.

"Okay." He scooped her up into his arms. "To your room." In the middle of Verity's sitting area, he stopped. "I just realized you don't even have a TV in here. The last nanny who stayed here had her own."

"I don't need a television. I don't watch it very much."

He looked surprised. "You don't watch reality shows?"

She shook her head.

"Or the Discovery Channel?"

Again she shook her head and gave him a little smile. "I can always find so many things I'd rather do. Listening to music, especially." She pointed to the CD player on her night stand. "Now *that* I can't do without."

"You can use the stereo system in the great room anytime you want."

"I noticed you have an extensive collection of Beatles music."

"Sure do. Play it anytime."

"That's kind of you, Mr. Montgomery. I just might."

"It's Leo," he said gruffly.

They'd never really addressed that issue. Jolene had introduced her to her employer as Verity the first time they'd met, but she'd always thought of him as Mr. Montgomery . . . on purpose. Today, however, everything seemed to have changed.

"Leo," she repeated softly.

"Vewitee wead me a stowy now?" Heather asked, laying her head on her dad's shoulder.

"One story coming right up," Verity assured her.

A short time later Leo stood beside the rocking chair as Verity sat with Heather, rocked and read her a favorite Dr. Seuss book. Heather's eyes were almost closed as they finished, and Leo lifted her from Verity's lap and placed her in her crib.

Then he leaned down to her, kissed her

forehead and said, "Good night, baby."

The huskiness in his voice tightened Verity's throat and she didn't know why. Maybe because Sean was gone. Maybe because her relationship with her father was strained. Maybe because she suddenly felt so alone.

Standing, she took a deep breath and said, "Nighty-night, Heather. I'll see you in the morning," and went to the door.

Leo joined her in the hall.

For a few moments they just stared at each other and a hum of attraction seemed to grow louder and stronger between them. They were standing very close, the toes of Leo's boots almost touching the toes of her sneakers. He towered a good six inches above her. When she looked up into his blue eyes, her tummy fluttered and her pulse raced. In fact, she almost felt as if she couldn't catch her breath. Leo didn't touch her, and she so wished he would. He looked as if he wanted to. He looked as if he wanted to kiss her.

With a shake of his head, he blew out a breath. "Do you feel safe here in this house with me?" he asked.

"Yes!"

"I didn't realize until tonight how this could look. Your staying here, I mean."

"I'm your nanny and housekeeper. Nannies often live in the residence where they take care of the children."

"That's true, but usually there's a wife. I don't want to compromise your reputation."

"I know who I am. I know why I'm here. What other people think really doesn't matter to me. Does it matter to you?"

"No, what other people think has never bothered me."

"Then we're fine," she said brightly. "There's nothing to be concerned about."

But the expression on his face as well as the wild beating of her heart told her that wasn't true. Besides that, if he knew how terrifically attracted she was to him, he might fire her. She liked this job, and she was beginning to like Avon Lake.

Tomorrow was Saturday, and to steer toward a safer subject, she asked, "Will you be going to the boatyard tomorrow?" He had worked the last three Saturdays she'd been here.

"For a few hours. I realized today I haven't been spending enough time with my daughter. That's going to have to change."

"I usually have breakfast for Heather around eight-thirty. Do you want to join us?"

After a pause he said, "Yes. I'll go to the boatyard afterward." There was an intensity in his gaze when he looked at her that excited her more than she wanted to admit. That excitement was as scary as the loneliness she'd felt as she'd watched Leo put his daughter to bed.

"I'll see you in the morning, then," she murmured.

When she turned to go, he finally touched her. His hand clasped her arm, and the feel of his hot skin on hers sent tingles through her whole body.

"Thank you for taking care of Heather so well today."

"It's my job."

Releasing her, he nodded. "I'll see you in the morning."

Then she was walking down the hall into the great room, bypassing the kitchen and heading to her suite. Today Leo Montgomery had become more than her employer. She wasn't sure how their relationship had changed, but she knew she had to be careful or she'd get hurt all over again.

Chapter Two

Verity was selecting clothes from her closet when she heard Heather on the baby monitor chattering to her stuffed animals. Smiling, she pulled on indigo jeans and zipped them, then grabbed a T-shirt that had seen many washings. The soft, blue cotton fell practically to her thighs. Comfort had always come first with her, certainly before fashion or trends or what anyone thought a girl *should* wear. Climbing trees, riding bikes and playing baseball with Sean had always led her to choose practical clothes.

Heather's babblings were getting louder now, and Verity left her room and headed for the little girl's. In the past, Leo had gone to work before she was up. Last night she'd had a restless night, reliving those moments when they'd stood so close, when she'd thought she'd seen something in his eyes that had made her heart jump so fast. This morning, though, in the light of day, she just chalked it all up to her imagination.

Heather stood up in her crib when she saw Verity, grinning from ear to ear. She stuffed a pink elephant — her toy of choice this week — under one arm.

"Good morning, honey," Verity said, scooping the little girl up into her arms. "I'm hoping that big bed your daddy ordered soon arrives. I'm afraid you're going to crawl out of this one."

"I cwawl out," Heather parroted, swinging Nosy by his trunk.

"Let's brush your teeth. Then you can decide what you want for breakfast."

"Waffles wif bluebewies," she said as if she'd been thinking about it all night.

Laughing, Verity shook her head. "You've had those every day this week."

"Waffles wif bluebewies," Heather repeated.

"Okay. I'm sure you'll get tired of them eventually."

Cooking was a pastime Verity enjoyed. She and Sean and her father had always shared the chore. After she'd gotten her own apartment in college, she'd found experimenting could be fun. Now she was glad she had. Heather could be a picky eater, and coming up with fun and playful ways to serve food was always a challenge.

Fifteen minutes later, teeth brushed, dressed in pink overalls and a matching shirt, Heather ran ahead of Verity to the kitchen. The bandage on her forehead was still in place and she wasn't paying any attention to it.

Verity hadn't seen any sign of Leo, but he might be working in his office in the pool house. She'd just started a pot of coffee brewing when a deep male voice made her jump. "Good morning."

Her hand over her heart, she swiveled toward the back door that led to the patio, pool and pool house. "Mr. Montgomery. I was going to call you when breakfast was ready."

He was carrying a folded sheet of paper in his hand. "It's Leo, remember?"

Oh, she remembered.

Without waiting for her response, he went on, "I thought I'd spend some time with Heather while you make breakfast. I realized yesterday I need to give her more attention."

Verity remembered how Heather had clung to her when Leo had arrived home to take her to the doctor. "I imagine it's difficult being a single parent."

"Funny," Leo said almost to himself, "I don't think of myself as single. But, yes, it is tough. After Heather's mother died, I guess I took refuge in work because Jolene was around to help me with Heather . . . or the nanny of the day. But yesterday when you called and said that Heather was hurt, I realized how very little I have to do with her day-to-day care."

"You're running a business."

"Yes, I am. Montgomery Boats will be her future, if she wants it. But in the meantime, I want to make sure I'm in her life."

Suddenly Heather ran to Verity with her coloring book. "Look what *me* did." She held up a page she had colored. Staying within the lines wasn't a concept she understood yet, but she knew her colors, and she'd used a lot of them on the page.

When Verity glanced at Leo, she saw the expression on his face and she realized he wished Heather had come to him.

"What a wonderful picture!" Verity exclaimed. "Show your daddy."

Looking puzzled for a moment, Heather tentatively held up the page to him. Verity could see Leo's uncertainty in exactly what to say or do. Then he crouched down, put his arm around his daughter, and offered, "That's a great blue dog. I bet he lives in the same place as pink elephants."

"Like Nosy," Heather decided.

"Just like Nosy."

"Heather insists she wants blueberry waffles for breakfast. Is that all right with you? I could scramble some eggs, too."

"It's been a long time since I had more than coffee for breakfast. Why don't I make the eggs?"

"Are you sure you want to help?"

He pulled one of the chairs over to the counter. "Sure. Heather can help, too. Heather, do you want to learn to crack an egg?"

"I wanna cwack *lots* of eggs," Heather said so fast, Verity could hardly catch it.

As Leo took the carton from the refrigerator, he replied, "I think we'll start with one."

Verity couldn't help but watch Leo as he made an effort to give Heather the attention he'd mentioned. He even let her stir the eggs with a fork. After a while, though, she tired of the process and told him, "I'm gonna color now." Leo lifted her down, and she went over to her miniature table and chairs to do just that.

When he frowned, Verity assured him, "Her attention span for most things is about ten minutes, unless it's something she's really into. Coloring is one of those things. Playing with blocks is another."

"Maybe she *will* grow up to want to design boats and build ships."

"Or houses or bridges or skyscrapers," Verity offered.

"I got it. I have to keep an open mind."

They smiled at each other and Verity felt all quivery inside. Leo's smile faded as he gazed at her, and the magnetic pull between them almost seemed to tug her toward him.

Then she remembered what he'd said earlier. *I don't think of myself as single.* That obviously meant he still thought of himself as married.

The timer beeped, signaling the first waffle was finished. Verity focused all of her attention into lifting the top of the iron, carefully removing the waffle and ladling in the next one.

The silence in the kitchen grew awkward until she finally asked, "When did you begin designing boats?"

"When I was ten."

She glanced at him. "What inspired you to do that?"

"My father. He didn't design boats, but he built them from someone else's plans. I spent every spare moment I could with him at the boatyard. I loved going out on the water with him, too. He had a real respect for the sea and taught me how to read it."

"Read it?" That idea fascinated her.

"Anyone can learn to pilot a boat. In-

41

struments these days make the experience almost a no-brainer. But there are still times when the color of the sky, the direction of the clouds, the scent of the water can tell a pilot the story as well as instruments can."

After Leo took a frying pan from the cupboard, he poured the eggs into it. The scent of the sweet waffles with blueberries, the aroma of coffee brewing, the eggs cooking in the skillet filled the kitchen along with the sound of Heather humming as she colored. The scene was so domestic it took Verity aback for a second. It was almost like a dream she'd had a week ago — a dream in which she'd had a home and a place to belong. But she really *didn't* belong here with Leo.

Did she?

Whatever she was feeling toward Leo Montgomery was probably all one-sided, and she'd better put the brakes on it. As his nanny, she was convenient right now. When he no longer needed her, he wouldn't hesitate to say goodbye, just as Matthew had.

Snatching a topic, any topic, she asked Leo, "How about your mother? Did she like boats and the water, too?"

Leo cast her a sideways glance. "Not on

your life. Mom's a high-heels, I-don't-want-to-get-my-hair-wet kind of person. She's never wanted anything to do with the boatyard or the business."

"Your sister told me she lives in Avon Lake, but she's away now."

"Lives in Avon Lake," Leo repeated. "Officially, I guess. She has an apartment, but rarely uses it for more than a few weeks at a time. She's become a world traveler."

"You come from such an interesting family."

He laughed. "That's one way of putting it. How about you?"

"Me?"

"Yes. Your parents. What do they do?"

Lifting the waffle iron before the timer went off, she saw the pastry was golden brown. Thankful she could stall for a little time to figure out what to say, she transferred it to a plate and decided to give an honest, short version. "My mother died when my brother and I were born. Sean and I were twins. Dad raised us. He's an accountant."

"A twin! That's great. What does your brother do?"

After Verity swallowed hard, she managed to say, "I lost Sean last January to a skiing accident." She went to pick up the ladle, but a blur of tears made her fumble it and drop it on the floor.

Leo stooped at the same time she did. His fingers brushed hers, and he took the ladle from her hand. When they both straightened, they were standing much too close, and he was looking down at her with so much compassion she couldn't blink away the tears fast enough.

"I'm sorry, Verity."

Embarrassed by the emotion she couldn't quell, she turned away from him toward the counter and took a few deep breaths. When she felt Leo's hand on her shoulder, she almost stopped breathing altogether.

"I'm okay," she murmured, feeling foolish.

Gently he nudged her around to face him. "No, you aren't. And I understand why. I know what loss feels like. Losing a spouse, losing a twin . . . Those are bonds that aren't easily broken."

"I don't want the bond to be broken," she admitted. "Not ever." Suddenly she realized that's the way Leo probably felt about his wife. "The eggs are going to burn," she whispered.

"Can't let that happen," he said, and

stepped away from her to tend to his part of the breakfast while she picked up a paper towel to wipe waffle batter from the floor.

Putting the breakfast on the table took little effort, but Verity busied herself with it as Leo helped Heather get settled on her booster seat.

Heather pointed to her waffle and looked up at Verity. "Please make a face."

The first day Verity had made the waffles for Heather, she wasn't sure if she was going to eat them. But after Verity had used syrup and a dab of butter to make a face on the waffle, Heather had eaten the whole thing. Now Verity fashioned a face again as Heather giggled and Leo looked on, making her feel self-conscious.

Suddenly there was a beep-beep-beep, and Verity realized it came from Leo's pocket.

After he answered his cell phone, he said, "Jolene. Hi. What's up? No, I'm not at the boatyard yet. I'm still at home having breakfast."

His sister must have made some comment about that because he explained, "I just needed some time with Heather. She hurt herself yesterday, and I realized I haven't been around very much." Then he

45

explained what had happened.

After a long pause he responded, "I'm going to the boatyard as soon as I'm finished. I'm sure Heather would love it if you would pick her up and take her to the arts festival at the lake."

Today artists would have their work displayed all around Avon Lake. There would be vendors with various foods, activities for kids and wandering musicians. Verity had thought about taking Heather there herself.

Now she said to Leo, "I'd be glad to take Heather and meet Jolene there. I want to go, too."

After Leo relayed what Verity had said to his sister, he asked Verity, "Around ten at the Shakespeare statue?"

Verity nodded. "Sounds good."

Leo closed the phone, reattached it to his belt and asked, "Are you sure you don't mind driving Heather there?"

"I don't mind. Really. I was planning to go after you got home."

"Will you buy a painting?" he asked jokingly.

"Actually, I might, if I see something I like. If that's okay with you. I mean, hanging it."

"I'm not a landlord who's going to keep

your security deposit if you put too many holes in the walls." His blue eyes were amused.

"I've just never been in this kind of position before," she said truthfully. "I don't know the rules."

"No rules, Verity. As long as you put Heather first, that's all that matters."

He was absolutely right on that score. She *would* put Heather first, of course, and try to block Leo Montgomery from her dreams.

Leo parked in a lot near the lake. As he'd sat in his office, studying each page of the new sales brochure, he hadn't been able to keep his mind on it. He hadn't been able to keep his mind off Verity. So he'd put in two hours, then driven to the festival.

His life had become a treadmill of work, putting Heather to bed now and then, sleep and more work. Even before Carolyn died, he'd started putting in longer hours. Had it been because of her remoteness? Had it been because he'd sensed she was keeping something from him?

She'd been keeping something from him all right . . . for three months — her brain tumor.

No point in thinking about that now. No

point in thinking about how her lack of trust had seemed like a betrayal, how her independence might have cost her her life sooner than was necessary.

The day couldn't have been any sunnier, sometimes unusual in this part of Texas where cloudy skies and rain could prevail in December. The lake was blue and the scents on the breeze from food vendors were enticing.

His boots cut a path through the grass as he observed everything going on. Avon Lake was a Texas town through and through. Yet the college, and the influence of the bard who had written sonnets and plays, brought a uniqueness to the community that wasn't easy to describe. The statue of Shakespeare himself on the shores of the lake was a roost for birds, true. But it was also a reminder there was an aspect of life that had to do with poetry, artistry and creation that humans couldn't do without.

When had he even thought about that statue?

Around the lake, artists displayed their paintings on easels, pegboards and some on more elaborate contraptions. Some of the displays were adorned with Christmas wreaths or signs of the season. The past two years Jolene had bought Heather Christmas presents when she'd gone shopping for her boys. This year, Leo decided, he would find presents for Heather himself.

He'd gone a quarter of the way around the lake when he spotted Verity. She wore an oversize green sweater over her jeans. Although the outfit seemed to be an attempt to hide womanly attributes, he found it only enhanced them. The cable knit lay softly over her breasts, the breeze blowing it against her body, delineating her slim waist. With her hair tied back in a ponytail, her face tilted curiously to one side as she studied a painting, the sun glinting on her glasses, Leo found himself eager to talk to her again. There was something about Verity Sumpter that was strangely appealing.

Coming up to stand beside her, he nonchalantly slid his hands into his jeans pockets. "Interpretable?" he asked wryly, as he gazed with her at the swirls of color and motion.

After a quick glance at him, she laughed. "I'm not sure. I do think it would clash with everything else you'd put with it, though."

Leo chuckled, too, then looked at her.

When their gazes met, Leo felt a tightening in his chest, and he didn't understand it at all. "Are you an art connoisseur?"

"Hardly. I like Victorian cottages, landscapes and paintings that take me away to someplace I want to be."

"Have you found any here today?" Blood was rushing through him faster now, and he chalked that up to his almost jog around the lake.

"A few. Have you seen Heather?"

"Not yet."

"The last time I spotted her she was at a stand making huge bubbles in the air. The wand was almost as big as she was."

"Did you eat lunch yet? We can grab a hot dog while we're looking." Then he stopped. "Unless you want to do this on your own."

She shrugged as if it didn't matter one way or the other. "I've made the rounds and I'm trying to decide between two paintings. A hot dog might help me make the decision."

For whatever reason, Verity Sumpter made him smile. She did more than that, he realized, as his gaze settled on her lips and he felt a pang of desire so strong he didn't think he'd ever felt anything quite like it before.

"Come on," he said evenly, nodding toward a concession truck that sold cold drinks, soft pretzels and hot dogs.

Strumming his guitar and dressed in purple velvet, a wandering minstrel serenaded them with a rendition of "Greensleeves" as they stood in line. Minutes later they each held hot dogs and sodas and went to stand under a pecan tree. When Verity took a one-handed bite of her hot dog, mustard caught on her upper lip. With her hands full and a napkin tucked under the bun, she couldn't wipe it away.

Not sure what possessed him, Leo set his soda between branches on the tree and caught the dab of mustard with his thumb. The touch of his skin on hers was electric, and her brown eyes widened with the jolt of it. What was it about Verity that stirred him up so?

She didn't look away, and he couldn't seem to, either. When he leaned toward her, she tipped up her chin.

All he had to do was bend his head —

"Verity. Hey, Verity," a male voice called.

A good-looking young man who appeared to be in his late twenties approached them. He had long, russet hair that curled over his collar and was brushed to one side. His green eyes targeted Verity and his smile was all for her.

As if she couldn't quite tear her gaze from Leo's, she blinked, breaking the spell. Her cheeks reddened slightly.

The man was approaching them then, and she was smiling at him. "Hi."

The guy's smile widened as he came up to them and stood very close to Verity. Much too close, Leo thought.

"Have you seen Charley's work? It's the style you said you liked — mountains and trees that make you feel as if you're right there."

Leo suddenly wondered if Verity had been dating this man. She could be, and he'd never know. He had no right to know.

"I've seen it," she offered with some excitement.

After another look at Leo and their half-eaten hot dogs, the young man gave Verity a slow smile. "I don't want to intrude." He rested his hand lightly on Verity's shoulder. "I'll see you Tuesday night. You can tell me then whether you bought the painting or not."

After the young man walked away, the silence that fell over Leo and Verity was louder than any of the noises around them. As they finished their hot dogs, Leo was very aware, again, that he was twelve years older than Verity and he had no business thinking about kissing her.

Yet questions rolled in his head, and he asked one of them. "Are you dating him?"

Her gaze flew to Leo's. "What made you think I was?"

Leo shrugged. "Maybe it was more his attitude than yours. If he hasn't asked you out, it won't be long until he does." He didn't like the idea of that — the idea of Verity and that guy in a dark movie theater, in a car or somewhere more intimate.

"I haven't dated much since . . ." She stopped and looked out over the lake. "Sean was protective of me. He screened my dates," she confided with a small smile.

Leo liked the idea of her having a protective brother who'd looked out for her. "Did you always go along with his advice?"

"I should have. Sean didn't like the man I was dating last fall, but I wouldn't listen. When you have a twin, a twin as close as Sean and I were, sometimes it's hard to distinguish your ideas from theirs, where you leave off and they begin. Being a twin is a constant battle to be yourself yet hold strong the bonds that bind you together. So I didn't listen to his advice about Matthew."

"What happened?"

"We'd been dating a few months when Sean was in the skiing accident. Afterward, I . . . I sort of withdrew. I just couldn't wrap my mind around the fact that Sean wasn't here anymore."

"That's not unusual," Leo offered, seeing her sadness, knowing what he had felt after he'd lost Carolyn.

"Matthew didn't understand that I just wasn't in the mood to go to parties or even the movies. Whenever I was with him, he didn't want to hear about Sean or how much I missed him. After a few weeks he told me that he needed to date somebody who was a lot more fun, and I realized my brother had been right about him all along."

Angry for her, Leo could have called this Matthew a few choice names, but he refrained because he could see how hurt Verity had been that someone she'd loved had deserted her at a low time in her life.

Verity had finished her hot dog and now took a sip of her soda. "How did you meet your wife?"

"I built a customized boat for her father. She came along to see the design, and that was that."

"So . . . you believe in love at first sight?" Verity asked curiously.

"I don't know if it was love at first sight. Carolyn was a beautiful, sophisticated, poised woman who could turn a man's head. She turned mine."

It wasn't until later that Leo had realized there was an aloofness about Carolyn that he could never really break through. Maybe that was the poise he had seen at first. That aloofness had never completely crumbled and had kept a barrier of sorts between them.

"Let's walk," Leo said gruffly.

When Verity glanced at him, there were questions in her eyes, but he didn't want her to ask them.

They hadn't gone very far when a little whirlwind came barreling toward Verity. It was Heather, all smiles and giggles and excitement.

Wrapping her arms around Verity's legs, she looked up at her with the exuberance of a three-year-old. "Looky. Looky. I got painted."

Without hesitation, Verity sank down onto one knee before Heather who had a cluster of daisies painted on her cheek.

"You look beautiful," Verity exclaimed, and Leo's chest tightened at the sight of this nanny and his daughter bonding. It was evident Heather absolutely adored Verity.

Heather grabbed Verity's hand. "You get painted, too."

Rising to her feet, Verity began, "Oh, I don't know . . ."

"Let yourself go today," Leo advised her, guessing that wasn't something Verity did often.

Jolene and her two boys had come up behind Heather. Jolene's hair was blonder than his. At five-four, she was about twenty pounds overweight, but she was his sister, so Leo simply didn't care. Jolene liked to cook and bake. Everything she did, she did with gusto.

Now she told Verity, "They'll paint whatever you want — from flowers to kittens to parrots. And it washes off."

"Are you going to do it, too?" Verity asked with a twinkle in her eye.

"I could be talked into it. But my boys won't stand still long enough for me to have it done."

"I can take the boys and Heather over to the clown with the balloons if you really want to," Verity offered.

Jolene's two boys, Randy and Joe, seemed to like the idea. Randy, the eight-year-old who was three years older than his brother, Joey, added, "And if Mom's not done until we get the balloons made we can play croquet. Kids are doing it over there." He pointed to an open area at the southern end of the lake.

"You're going to have your hands full," Leo warned her.

"They'll be fine as long as we keep busy."

Leo cupped Verity's elbow. Again, he felt a longing inside. But he realized it wasn't only desire.

Trying to ignore whatever it was, he decided, "First, you get your turn getting painted, then I'll help you look after the kids."

When Verity gazed up at him, everyone else around the lake seemed to disappear. The overwhelming desire to kiss her overtook him once more.

Releasing her elbow, he decided to keep his distance and concentrate on the kids.

Something had happened to him since Verity's call yesterday. He felt as if he was reacting and responding and living again.

All of it had something to do with this nanny. He just had to figure out where she fit into his life . . . if she fit in at all.

Chapter Three

Before Verity turned in for the night, she decided to make herself a cup of cocoa. Her mind was racing and she knew sleep wouldn't come quickly . . . not tonight. She'd enjoyed the afternoon with Leo and Heather so much she couldn't get it out of her mind.

She was stirring the mixture of chocolate and milk in the saucepan on the stove when she heard the sliding glass doors in the dining room open and close. Her heart rate sped up, and when Leo came into the kitchen, she told herself to calm down. This afternoon had meant the world to her. She'd had fun for the first time in a long time. However, she'd also realized her attraction to Leo wasn't something she could ignore easily.

Dressed in a denim shirt and black jeans, his tawny hair tousled, she wondered what had brought him back into the house. After he'd put Heather to bed, he'd told her he was going to work in the pool house for a while. The pool house was his office, and she knew he had a baby monitor in there like the one in her room so he could hear his daughter if she awakened or called for him.

"Is Heather awake?" She looked toward the little girl's room.

"Nope. Not after the afternoon she had. I wouldn't be surprised if she sleeps later than usual in the morning, too. I picked up my e-mail, and Jolene sent me these. I thought you might like to see them."

"What are they?"

"Pictures from this afternoon that Jolene took with her digital camera. I just printed them out."

Verity gestured toward the pot on the stove. "Would you like some hot chocolate?"

After a glance at the pot, he met her gaze. "Sure. That doesn't look like the powdered stuff I make in the microwave."

"It's not. It's the real thing. I found the chocolate in a candy store in town."

He was carefully studying her as if he was trying to figure something out. Unsettled by his intense focus on her, she reached for two mugs from the mug tree in the corner. Setting them on the counter, she poured the chocolate into them and carried them to the table.

Leo followed her, then lowered himself into a chair and spread out the pictures.

There were four sheets of them with four pictures on each. Heather was the star of all the photos, whether she was gazing up at a strolling minstrel, learning how to play croquet with Verity, or licking her fingers from the cotton candy Leo held in one hand as he stooped down to her to give her another taste.

"These are great," Verity said, letting her chocolate cool a bit. "You ought to frame a few and put them in the great room."

"Maybe I will."

"Do you keep a photo album?"

"No, I haven't had the time. All of the pictures are in a box in the closet." Lifting his mug to his lips, he took a swallow.

Verity was mesmerized by the crow's feet at Leo's eyes . . . the shadow of beard on his jaw . . . his strong neck muscles as he drank the cocoa. A trill of attraction spun in her tummy.

Didn't she know better than to weave dreams? Didn't she know better than to think Leo Montgomery could be interested in her? He moved in the country club set. He'd had a wife who had been sophisticated and everything Verity wasn't.

With a smile, he set his mug on the table. "This is great!"

She felt inordinately pleased that he

liked the concoction. "It's good with a little bit of coffee mixed in, too."

Again he was studying her. Yesterday, as well as today, he looked at her as if he hadn't really seen her before. That was odd since she'd been here almost a month.

"Did you hang the painting you bought?" he asked.

"Not yet. I need a hammer and a nail."

"I think I can come up with those. Do you want to hang it now?"

"*I* can do it, if you have something else you'd rather be doing."

Standing, he went to the kitchen closet, took a hammer and a box of nails from the top shelf. "It would be best to make sure the nail goes into a stud. I can do that for you."

A few minutes later, they were standing in Verity's sitting room, and she was showing Leo the wall where she'd like to hang the painting. It was an ocean scene at sunrise — pink, purple and gold spread across the morning sky as two horses grazed on tufts of sea grass along the beach.

After Leo made sure he knew where she wanted the painting, he rapped against the wall with his knuckles until the sound was slightly different. Then he hammered a nail right in. Taking the painting from her, he found the middle of the wire hanger and slipped it over the nail.

"What do you think?" he asked, stepping back, his arm brushing hers.

"I like it. It makes me want to go riding on the beach."

He was looking at *her* now, rather than at the painting. "Do you ride?"

"Just for fun. I never took lessons."

"There's a natural rhythm to riding. Some people catch on to it, some don't."

They were standing close together. So close Verity could see a scar on Leo's cheek, right above his beard line. So close that she could smell the maleness of him. So close that she could feel his heat.

When he reached out and traced the daisy that had been painted on her cheek, she trembled.

"Heather didn't want me to wash off her flower tonight." His voice was husky.

"This will fade away when I get my shower."

His thumb traced the petals of the flower. "So soft," he murmured, and her heart began galloping as it had never galloped before.

There was a look in Leo's eyes she'd never seen before. Although Matthew had kissed her many times, his kisses had been eager, enthusiastic, intended to convince her to want more. She hadn't wanted more with him. It was really the bottom-line reason they'd broken up. She hadn't been ready to have sex and he'd moved on. She'd grown up believing she wanted to save herself for the one, perfect relationship . . . the one man she'd love for the rest of her life.

Leo was a man. All man. The desire in his eyes spoke of a raw hunger that should have scared her because she was a virgin and he was experienced. Yet she wasn't afraid. She was curious.

The periphery of her life fell away. There was only that hunger in Leo's eyes and her desire to satisfy it. When he bent his head, he gave her time to back away. But she could no more back away than she could forget about the brother she'd lost. Leo's lips sealed to hers, and everything about her life turned and shifted. This man and his need awakened passion in her she'd never known she possessed. As her arms went around his neck, his mouth opened over hers.

Leo's kiss stunned her and swirled her into sensation that left her breathless and reaching for more. When her hands slipped into Leo's hair, she couldn't seem to get close enough to him. A groan sounded deep in his throat as his tongue stroked hers, as the kiss lasted for an eternity, as she responded to him in the way a woman responds to a man. Leo Montgomery stirred up excitement she'd never known.

Then suddenly his arms dropped, and his lips broke from hers. His hold on her shoulders loosened as he pushed her away.

"This is wrong," he muttered, his face taking on a stony expression.

Unable to find many words, she asked, "Why?"

"There are so many reasons I can't even count them all. First of all, I'm your employer. Second, I'm twelve years older than you are. Third . . ." He stopped.

"Third?" Unfortunately she guessed what was coming.

"Third, this isn't what I want. And you can't tell me it's what you want, either. Attraction is two parts chemistry, one part proximity and no parts common sense. I'm old enough to know common sense has to reign. Let's just forget that kiss ever happened."

For the first time in her life, Verity had had a taste of true desire. For the first time in her life, she felt something for a man that went beyond attraction and chemistry and reason. Nevertheless, from the look in Leo's eyes she could see that he was convinced they were wrong for each other. Words wouldn't convince him otherwise, and she didn't know if anything else would, either. Tears welled up and she quickly blinked them away.

Leo must have seen them. "If you want to leave, I'll understand."

"I don't want to leave. I like taking care of Heather." To herself she added, *And I like being near you.* But she didn't dare say that aloud. He'd fire her for sure.

He went to the door. "I'll be taking Heather to a puppet show at the mall tomorrow. Do you have plans for your day off?"

No, she didn't. But she was going to pretend she did. That just seemed to be best. She'd make herself scarce, no matter what time he left or returned. "I'm going to Freeport to shop for Christmas. Do you decorate for the holidays? I can pick up some festive arrangements, maybe a door hanging for you."

He looked blank. "I haven't decorated since . . ." He stopped and cleared his throat. "A few decorations would probably be good for Heather. I'll get a tree closer to Christmas." Studying her closely, he added, "It's your day off. You don't have to be thinking about Heather or the house. I can always pick up a few decorations."

"I really don't mind. Christmas is a special time for children. I want it to be special for Heather this year."

Reaching into his back pocket, he extracted his wallet, took out a few bills and handed them to her. "If you want to pick out decorations for the house, go ahead."

As she took the bills, his hand closed over hers. His fingers were strong and firm. His gaze fell to her lips —

But then he released her and backed away. "Have a good day tomorrow," he said gruffly, then turned and left her room.

The magnetic pull between them had been so very strong since Friday. Had he left so abruptly because he wanted to kiss her again? Or did he simply regret everything that had happened between them?

Sinking into one of the chairs in her sitting room, she stared at the painting he'd helped her hang on the wall.

She'd better close and lock her heart if she wanted to stay employed here. She'd better remember Leo Montgomery was off-limits. What she remembered, however, was his kiss and the way it had made her feel.

Staring at the painting, she could imagine herself and Leo on those horses at the beach. When she closed her eyes, she blanked out the picture, knowing her imagination would only bring her heartache.

In the craft store on Sunday afternoon, Verity heard the rat-a-tat of rain on the roof. Selecting various items, she lowered them into her basket. She'd decided creating decorations might be more enjoyable than buying them. More economical, too. Not that Leo had to worry about that. But she and Heather could work on them together, and that would be fun.

She'd just arranged a pine-cone garland in the basket when a lilting musical tone emanated from her purse. It had to be the wrong number — not many people had her cell phone number. When she checked the small window, her chest tightened a little. It was her dad.

"Did I catch you at a bad time?" Gregory Sumpter asked.

She pulled her basket into an alcove at the end of the row. "No, this is fine. I was shopping."

"For you or your new job?"

"For my job."

"On a Sunday?"

She didn't want to tell him how her days off seemed endless. She didn't want to tell him how she was feeling because she knew exactly how *he* was feeling. He missed Sean. Sean had been his golden child. Sean had been the male heir. Though Sean had taken engineering in college, her father had still held fast to the dream that he'd take over his three hardware stores someday, making them an even bigger father-and-son success.

"Did you have a reason for calling, Dad?" He didn't call her often. When he wasn't working, he closed himself in his study, staring at old photo albums, polishing Sean's trophies.

"I wondered if you were going to come home for Christmas."

Thanksgiving had come and gone without a phone call from her dad. She'd called him the week before a few times, not wanting to let the holiday pass without connecting, but he hadn't returned those calls.

"I don't know yet," she told him now. "I haven't thought much about Christmas." If she had dinner on the holiday with her father, they'd sit across the table from each other, not saying a word. She thought about being around Heather and watching the little girl's joy.

Being around Leo, too? a little voice inside her heart asked.

"Did you have anything special in mind?" In spite of her dad's remoteness, she still wanted to reach out to him. They didn't have relatives nearby. Her father had been an only child. Her mother had a sister, but she lived in Boston and they only saw her every few years. Verity wrote to her often and they called each other every couple of months, but actual visits were few and far between.

"No, nothing special. In fact, if you don't think you'll be coming home, I might drive to Corpus Christi. Ted Cranshaw — I knew him when I was in the Navy — just bought a big place there. He said if I wasn't doing anything on Christmas, I should come over."

So her father really hadn't called to say he missed her. He really hadn't called to say he wanted her to come home for Christmas. He'd called to see if she was tied up, because if she was, then he could do his own thing. She didn't want him to ask her to come home only because he felt that he should.

Keeping disappointment and a world of hurt from her voice, she said evenly, "You go visit your friend, Dad. That's fine."

"Are you sure?"

Of course she wasn't sure. Holidays were meant for family. But family had to involve more than duty, and that seemed to be all that was left with her father. "I'm sure."

An awkward silence fell between them — a familiar, awkward silence. He cleared his throat. "Oh, I almost forgot. What about your mail? Should I forward that to you? You got a letter that looks very businesslike from some production company."

Probably the company that shot the commercial. That seemed like eons ago now. Anything about it reminded her of Sean and his grin as he'd given her a wolf whistle and a thumb's-up sign right before the shoot. It also brought back memories of Matthew and his absolute fascination with her new look. She wondered if she'd met him with her hair straight, glasses on her nose, would he even have given her a second look. Probably not.

Leo had given her a second look. When she relived that kiss —

"Verity?"

She couldn't believe how thoughts of Leo could distract her. "I'm here, Dad.

Don't worry about my mail. If you want to stick it all in an envelope and send it to me, that's fine."

"All right. That's what I'll do. Take care of yourself, Verity."

"I will. You take care, too."

When she closed her phone, tears came to her eyes that she couldn't will away.

On Monday morning Verity was folding laundry in the kitchen when Leo called around nine o'clock. He'd left for work before her alarm had gone off. She'd barely seen him yesterday after her trip to Freeport. Last night she'd worked on a paper for the class she was auditing, every once in a while hearing Heather's laughter, hearing Leo's deep baritone from the monitor, remembering their kiss.

Now she wondered why he was calling, since she rarely heard from him during working hours.

"How busy is your morning?" he asked.

"Just the usual chores and playtime with Heather. Why?"

"I have a favor to ask. I'd like to bring a client home for supper. I could take him to a restaurant, but Mr. Parelli is a family man. He has four kids of his own. I'll be piloting his cabin cruiser to Port Aransas in a week or so, and he's mentioned ordering another for his brother. Anyway, he talks about his kids all the time, and I thought he might like to meet Heather."

"What kind of dinner would you like me to prepare?" Leo was rarely home for supper. She usually left a plate for him in the refrigerator, and he ate when he got home.

"It doesn't have to be anything fancy," he added.

"I'll come up with something. But I will have to take Heather to the store. Is that all right with you?"

Leo had bought a second car seat for Verity's car, but she always let him know when she was taking his daughter someplace other than the preschool two mornings a week.

"That's not a problem. Just don't let her convince you to buy one of each kind of candy bar."

Verity laughed. "Don't worry. I have her almost convinced that granola bars are better."

After a brief silence, when neither knew exactly what to say, Leo broke it. "Thanks, Verity. Mr. Parelli is coming to Avon Lake this afternoon, so you can plan dinner for around six."

"I'll do that."

As Verity hung up, she thought about the menu. Glancing into the dining room, she realized she hadn't asked Leo if he wanted her to use the good china in the hutch, but she assumed she should.

There was something else she hadn't asked him. Did he want her to join them for dinner? If he and his client wanted to talk, she could distract Heather. She'd set a place for herself, and if he didn't want it there, she could take it away.

By 5:30 Verity thought she was ready. The table was set, the beef Stroganoff was simmering, the rice would be finished steaming in fifteen minutes. She'd dressed Heather in a pretty lilac flowered dress, and she'd taken more care with her outfit, choosing navy pants, a red knit top and a cotton camp shirt of navy and red. She'd even tied a jaunty red ribbon around her ponytail band. Whether she was serving or sitting down with Leo and Heather at dinner, she didn't want to embarrass him.

She'd just settled Heather on the floor of the great room with her coloring book and a plastic container full of crayons when the doorbell rang. Hurrying to the foyer, Verity answered it.

When she opened the front door, she

found a balding man with a round face who looked to be in his fifties. He was wearing a white polo shirt and tan cargo slacks with deck shoes.

"Mr. Parelli?" she asked, wondering why he was at the door alone.

He smiled at her. "That's me. Leo got an unexpected phone call he had to take, and I told him I could find my way here. He said he wouldn't be long."

"Come on in," she invited with a wave of her hand toward the great room. "I'm just keeping an eye on supper and playing with Heather."

As Mr. Parelli stepped over the threshold, she closed the door. "Leo said you have four children of your own. How old are they?"

"Twelve, ten, six and two," he responded with a friendly smile. "Two boys and two girls. I've got a diverse bunch. Mary and I started later in life than most, I guess. But the kids make every day an adventure."

"Leo told me he'll be delivering your boat to Port Aransas. Do you live there?"

"Unfortunately, no. We just have a small getaway house there. I live in Lake Jackson. When Leo brings the boat to Port Aransas, will you be coming with him?"

She doubted that. But before she had a

chance to say so, she heard a loud clatter in the great room, and Heather was running toward her, wailing, "My cwayons all spilled."

"If there's anything I can do to help, Mrs. Montgomery . . ." Mr. Parelli said.

Just as his words registered, the front door opened and Leo came in. "Hey, Tony. I see you found your way here."

"Sure did. Your wife and I are getting acquainted."

Heather was tugging on Verity's hand when Tony Parelli spoke, and she wasn't sure what to do. Stooping down, Verity picked up Heather and held her in her arms. "Just a minute, honey."

Leo looked from Verity to Mr. Parelli. "Tony, Verity isn't my wife. She's my nanny. Or rather, Heather's nanny."

An awkward silence seemed to reverberate from the foyer throughout the great room.

Finally, Tony Parelli gave a little shrug. "I see." His cheeks reddened slightly.

Totally embarrassed, Verity murmured, "Let me get Heather settled again, and then I'll put supper on the table."

"Will you be joining us?" Tony asked, obviously curious about their lifestyle. Verity saw Leo glance into the dining room and back at his daughter. "Yes, she will."

Why had Leo included her? Because she could tend to Heather? Or because he wanted Parelli to think they were a family, even if an unorthodox one?

Verity suddenly wished that was true.

Stepping closer to Verity, Leo took Heather from her arms. "Come on, kiddo. I'll keep her with us while you get supper out," he said to Verity with a cold look that she didn't understand.

For the most part, Verity kept quiet during dinner, simply taking care of Heather's needs. Tony addressed her specifically, once or twice. However, Leo's attitude was remote, and she wished she knew what he was thinking. Did this dinner with his client make him miss his wife even more?

When Verity offered to get Heather ready for bed, Leo politely thanked her. After she said good night to both men, she read Heather a story, then settled her in her crib for the night, Nosy tucked under her arm.

She'd just turned on her CD player in her sitting room and settled in an armchair with her knitting needles and yarn when there was a knock at her door.

Opening it, she saw Leo. "I think we

should talk. Come into the great room, would you?"

His gaze cut to the painting that she'd bought at the arts festival, and she knew he was remembering their kiss. She had the feeling he might never enter her sitting room again, at least not while she was in it.

After she followed him to the great room, he didn't sit and neither did she. Rather, he dug his hands deep into his pockets and asked, "Why did you lie to Parelli?"

The question was so far from anything she might have expected, all she could do was repeat, "Lie?"

"Yes. Obviously you told him something that gave him the impression you were my wife."

"Obviously I didn't do anything of the kind." Where she had been upset before, now she was angry. Why would Leo think she'd lied? "I'd never intentionally mislead *anyone.*"

Leo's narrowed gaze told her he didn't believe her.

"Mr. Parelli came to the door, I opened it and we started talking," she explained shortly. "I was trying to put him at ease. Then Heather spilled her crayons, he called me Mrs. Montgomery, and you walked in the door. I didn't have *time* to correct him."

"You could have said immediately that you weren't Mrs. Montgomery."

Had she hesitated? Had she liked the idea of the title? Or had she simply been so startled no correction had found its way to her tongue? "I'm sorry, Leo. I never meant to mislead your client. Believe me, I know my position here."

Before Leo could reproach her further, before she could wonder again about her own feelings on the subject, she turned her back on him and left the room.

Feeling more than attraction to Leo Montgomery wasn't acceptable, and she had to figure out what to do about it.

Chapter Four

As Verity walked down the tiled hall of the Arts and Sciences Building of Avon College the following evening, she thought about Leo and his reaction to what had happened with Mr. Parelli last night. Why had he ever thought she would lie? Where had that idea even come from?

She had never done anything that would give him the impression she wouldn't tell the truth.

Then again, they really didn't know each other very well.

Why did she want him to think only the best of her? Why did his opinion matter so much?

Arriving at Dr. Will Stratford's office door, she didn't answer the question. Tonight she was supposed to pick up forms to fill out for next semester.

The top portion of the door was plate glass and she could see into the professor's office. Dr. Stratford was sitting at the desk, bent over some papers. His gray hair was mussed and sticking up all over. His bow tie was askew as usual. His suspenders today were bright red. The professor had the reputation for being highly intelligent but a bit kooky and absent-minded. Retired now from the English Department, he helped out where needed, sometimes even giving guest lectures. He'd taught everything from Shakespeare to William Blake and Lord Byron.

When she rapped on the door, he looked up and then motioned her inside.

Standing when she entered, he pushed his wire-rim spectacles up higher on his nose. "Hello, Verity. It's good to see you again."

From the moment she'd met the grandfatherly Dr. Stratford, she'd felt as if she'd known him all her life. "I was hoping to catch you. I couldn't remember if you had office hours this evening."

"Have a seat," he said, gesturing to a chair. "I'm here more than I'm not."

"But you're retired!"

After she sat, he lowered himself into the old wooden chair on rollers behind his desk and grinned. "Retirement is for folks who don't love their work. They think by quitting it, they'll find happiness. I knew better. I have my hobbies, and my cat meows that I'm not home enough, but keeping busy will keep me young."

"You have a cat?" she asked, amused.

"Yes, indeed. Sheets is a gray tabby who is overweight and entirely spoiled. He rules my house. I only reside there."

She laughed.

"That's better," Dr. Stratford remarked.

"What do you mean?"

"You were looking much too serious when you knocked on my door."

"I was thinking about something . . . someone."

"Are you having a problem I could help with?"

"Oh, Dr. Stratford. If only."

"Call me Will," he suggested.

There was a kindness that emanated from Dr. Stratford that helped her relax whenever she spoke with him. He seemed to truly care about what mattered to her, whether it came to classes or family matters. In her first meeting with him she'd found herself telling him about Sean. He'd understood everything she was feeling, and a bond had formed between them.

Leo understood, too, a little voice whispered.

Will Stratford leaned forward a bit, his arms crossed on his desk. "Whatever the problem, it's distracting you," he noticed with concern.

That was certainly true. "It's my job,"

she answered vaguely.

"You took a position as an au pair, right?"

"Yes, that's right. And my boss —" She stopped abruptly.

Will straightened, uncrossing his arms and gazing at her steadily. "Is he mistreating you in any way?"

Seeing the concern in Professor Stratford's gaze, she hurried to correct the conclusion he'd jumped to. "No. Absolutely not. It's just . . ." She paused and then in a rush added, "I'm attracted to him. He's a widower, and I already love his little girl."

The teacher's expression relaxed, and he leaned back in his chair, making it creak. "Ah, I see. Is this attraction one-sided?"

When she thought about Leo's kiss, her cheeks caught fire. "I don't think so. It's just that I'm younger than he is, and I think he's still tied to the past."

"You mean his deceased wife?" Will asked, catching on quickly.

"Yes."

As soon as she'd uttered the word, she felt as if she'd betrayed some kind of confidence.

Will must have seen that because he hurried to assure her, "Verity, whatever we talk about in here, I will keep confidential. I'm your advisor. If you don't trust me, I can't advise you. In January you'll be starting your work in earnest. If this situation you're in is going to interfere with that, you should talk it through."

She knew he was right. "Nothing is going to interfere. I don't think Leo's ready for any type of romantic involvement."

After studying her carefully, Will's expression became sober. "Let me ask you something, Verity. You said this man is tied to his past. Are you tied to yours?"

The question took her aback. *Was* she tied to her past? Was she ready for a relationship? Or did she still expect men to walk out on her? Her dad had always been available for Sean, but she'd felt as if she were merely part of the package. Matthew had left when the going got rough. And Sean . . . he'd abandoned her, too, in a way. So even if she and Leo explored the attraction between them and found common ground, would *she* back away? Could she dare to dream that Leo would be different from her dad . . . from Matthew?

"I see that's a question you might have to think about."

"Yes, it is."

Taking a manila envelope from a stack on the side of his desk, Will opened it and took out a sheaf of papers. "Look over the catalog carefully, check out the classes listed here on early childhood education, and then fill out the paperwork." After he stuffed it all back in, he handed her the envelope. "Return them to me before Christmas, then we'll get your schedule moving for next semester."

Knowing she'd be late for class if she didn't leave, Verity stood and tucked the envelope under her arm. "Thank you for all your help."

"I don't help. I just listen and sort a bit." He stood, too. "In a little while I'll be sending you your official welcome letter for the new year. There will be another form for you to return to Student Affairs. Don't let it get lost in the Christmas shuffle."

"I won't."

With a wave, she left Will Stratford's office and hurried to her class. She didn't know how much auditing she'd be doing tonight. She'd be thinking about her ties to the past.

When Verity returned to Leo's house after her class, silence greeted her. She was both relieved and disappointed. After last night's fiasco, not seeing Leo lowered her stress level. On the other hand, she wished they could find an easy footing again.

If she checked on Heather, she might run into him.

Suddenly she didn't have to worry about running into him. He was standing there — in jeans, bare feet and an unbuttoned shirt.

"I was about to get a shower when I heard you come in. We need to talk."

His deep voice was sure and certain, and fear that he was going to fire her gripped her. After all, if he thought she'd lied —

"If you want to get your shower, I can wait." It wasn't in her nature to procrastinate or avoid the inevitable. But in this case . . .

"I don't want to wait."

As Leo approached her, trembling began deep inside of her and seeped through her body. She couldn't keep from responding to him even if she wanted to.

Taking a deep breath and squaring her shoulders, she stood up for herself. "I didn't lie last night, Leo. Mr. Parelli just jumped to the wrong conclusion."

"I know."

Those weren't the words she expected to hear. "You know? Did you talk with Mr. Parelli?"

Leo motioned toward the great room.

"Let's go in and sit down. There's something I want to tell you. It might help you understand why *I* jumped to the wrong conclusion."

The intensity in Leo's eyes gave her pause for a moment, but then she took a deep breath and began to slip her backpack from her shoulders.

Before she could, he caught it, his large hand grazing her arm. Enticing tingles ran through her from the heat of his touch.

"This weighs a ton," he complained with a small smile, as he hefted it onto the table.

"Not quite that much," she responded lightly, feeling almost buoyant because she didn't think this discussion was going to be about firing her.

"You're much stronger than you look, aren't you?" Leo asked, his gaze immobilizing her.

"I've never thought about it. I work out every morning. I have weights in my closet."

"I wasn't just talking about physical strength."

Leo was looking at her as if he admired her. She didn't think any man had looked at her quite that way before.

After he motioned her into the great

room, he followed her to the sofa.

When he sat beside her, she was much too cognizant of his unbuttoned shirt, his chest hair that was inviting her fingers to touch it. He seemed oblivious to his just-before-a-shower appearance and was totally focused on the conversation he wanted to have with her.

"Are you sure you don't want to get your shower?" Even his bare feet were sexy.

As if with a sudden flash of insight he was aware of the casualness of his attire, his fingers went to the buttons of his shirt and he quickly fastened them. "This won't take long," he said gruffly. "Then we can both call it a day."

Leo broke eye contact and then turned slightly to face her. "I hate lies," he said. "Purposeful lies *or* lies of omission. One's as bad as the other."

"I'd never lie to you."

His gaze was steady and piercing. "I haven't known you long enough to figure that out. Even in the short time I *have* known you, I've realized there are areas of your life you don't want to discuss. You seem secretive about your family."

"Not secretive. Some things just hurt too much to talk about."

Leo digested that. "All right. I can accept that. I don't talk about Carolyn much for many reasons. Some of those reasons caused me to jump to a mistaken conclusion last night."

"I don't understand."

"Carolyn lived with a secret for three long months without telling me." He raked his hand through his hair. "She started having headaches and kept that information from me. I was working a lot, keeping the business going through tough economical times. Later she made the excuse that that's why she hadn't revealed she was having headaches. That's why she hadn't revealed the family doctor had sent her to a neurologist. That's why, for three long months, she didn't tell me she had a brain tumor."

Verity was absolutely stunned, unable to imagine a wife withholding that information from a husband. "Why did she keep it from you?"

"I've asked myself that question at least a million times, because I didn't accept her answer when I put it to her. She explained her brain tumor was inoperable. She'd decided to accept the inevitable and live out whatever time she had with me and Heather in peace, adding as an afterthought that she was sure if she discussed her diagnosis with me, I'd want her to seek treatment — experimental treatment, any treatment — to keep her alive longer."

"She didn't want to live longer?"

"Carolyn was concerned with the quality of her life, not the quantity of it. You see, she didn't tell me about the diagnosis voluntarily. I came home and found her on the floor. She couldn't get up. That's how I knew something was terribly wrong, and her condition could no longer be her secret. A few months after that, she was gone."

"Leo, I'm so sorry."

He shook his head as if he didn't want her sympathy, and she realized he was a proud man. Because of that pride, the fact that his wife couldn't confide in him hurt even more deeply.

"I felt as if during those months she'd kept her condition hidden, we were living a lie."

"She was trying to protect you."

"No, I don't think she was. I think she was taking the time to decide what *she* wanted to do, and there was no room for my opinion. I don't think Carolyn even thought about what losing her mother would do to Heather."

He laid his hands on his thighs, stared

straight ahead, then turned back to Verity. "Anyway, that's why I jumped to the wrong conclusion last night."

She had to make something very clear to him. "I won't lie to you, Leo. Ever. And if there's something you want to ask me, ask me and I'll answer it."

"I'll start making a list," he joked with a wry smile that was meant to lighten the mood.

However, as their gazes met, locked and held, the mood wasn't lightened. Her attraction for him was met by his attraction for her, and the resulting collision sent sparks flying.

"I've tried to forget about kissing you." His voice was gruff, low and deep, and her tummy did a somersault.

"It was unforgettable," she murmured honestly, not knowing what else to say.

When he reached out, when his hand caressed her cheek, she knew she was in trouble. No man's touch had ever affected her as Leo's did. "Maybe I should find another job."

"Maybe you should," he agreed.

"Do you want me to leave?" she asked, knowing that would make all the difference.

His turmoil was evident in the darkening

of his blue eyes. "No, I don't. You're good with Heather, and you're good *for* her."

He dropped his hand to his side, and although he didn't move himself away physically, she felt him remove himself in every other way as he asked, "Do you want to stay?"

Although she was heading for deep water, although she didn't know if she could keep her boat afloat, she felt such a pull toward Leo she had to say, "Yes, I want to stay. I love taking care of Heather, and I feel safe here."

"Safe? How could you feel safe after I kissed you?"

"I knew what I was doing, Leo. If I had turned away, I have no doubt you would have left my room."

"You're so young," he growled with a shake of his head. "So naive."

That stirred up her temper. "I'm past the age of consent, and I can vote. I can also make my own decisions."

"But will they be wise ones, Verity? You and me . . . under the same roof —"

"I understand that I have the power to say yes as well as no. I understand the chemistry between us is powerful, but it doesn't change who we are."

Then, just as quickly as it had flared, the

moment of temper vanished, and she had to accept the fact that she *was* younger than Leo and terribly less experienced.

On the other hand, he had to realize she was more mature than he thought. "Having a male twin taught me a lot about men."

Leo was silent for a few long moments, but then he grumbled, "Maybe not enough." Rising to his feet he said, "You did a great job with dinner last night."

"Thank you," she murmured, knowing he was relegating her to an employee once more. He wanted to keep her in a box because he thought that was safer for both of them.

As they said their good nights and Leo left the great room, she didn't know how long she could stay in that box. She didn't know if she *wanted* to stay in that box. However, if she broke free, she had to make sure she was ready to face the consequences.

When the overnight package came for Leo the next day, Verity wasn't sure what to do. She could just let it sit until he came home, or she could call him and ask him if he needed it. As Heather pasted animal stickers onto a large piece of construction paper, Verity pulled the list of phone numbers from the refrigerator and dialed Leo's cell phone.

On the second ring, he clicked on. "Montgomery."

"Leo, it's Verity. An Express Mail package was delivered for you. It's from a company called Design Makers. Is it something you need?"

"Yes, it is. It's a computer program I've been waiting for. My secretary must have given them my home address." When he paused, she could hear the echo of voices, the sound of some type of machinery running.

"I'd like to have it as soon as possible, and I can't get away right now. I have a meeting in five minutes. How would you feel about dropping it off here?"

"I don't mind. But what about Heather?"

"I don't want Heather around the boatyard. I'll give Jolene a call and see if she can watch her for a little while. If she's not home, I'll call you back. I should be finished with the meeting by one."

"All right. If I don't hear from you, I'll be there then."

As Verity hung up, she had to admit she'd been curious about the boatyard.

Now maybe she'd get a glimpse of it.

A little before one, Verity took the side road that led to Montgomery Boat Company. It was a large complex, about twenty minutes outside of Avon Lake, near Surfside Beach. There was more than one building, and rising up to the side of the main plant she saw huge cranes. The layout of the complex told her Leo did a lot more than design boats.

Heading for the front of the smallest building, she passed rows of employees' cars. Finally she slid into a visitor's spot.

The office was pleasant and inviting with framed photographs of boats hanging on the blue walls. A nameplate on the secretary's desk said Mrs. MacLaren, and the woman smiled at Verity. Mrs. MacLaren, with her salt-and-pepper, short-cut hair, looked to be in her fifties.

Now she saw the package in Verity's hand. "Verity Sumpter?" she asked.

Verity nodded.

"Mr. Montgomery said to send you right in. That door over there." She pointed across the sitting area where gray-and-blue armchairs sat.

Verity made her way to the door and knocked.

Leo's deep "Yes?" affected her in a way

she couldn't quite explain.

When she opened the door, he was seated at his desk, surrounded by catalogs. Standing, he smiled. "Come on in."

"This complex is huge," she said as she stepped inside.

He laughed. "We build boats. They're big."

"I don't know what I expected."

"Maybe a little Mom and Pop shop and rowboats sitting around?"

She felt her cheeks redden.

"Sorry, I couldn't resist." He looked amused. "And it's not so far from the truth. That's how my grandfather started out — from birch hulls to fiberglass hulls."

She knew she looked blank.

"Would you like a tour?"

Laying the package on his desk, she asked, "You're not too busy?"

"I'm always busy." He motioned to the half sandwich on his blotter. "But since I didn't stop for lunch, I can take a break. Come on, I'll show you around."

Today Leo was dressed in jeans with a striped oxford shirt, the sleeves rolled up his forearms. As they left the office and went outside down a walk to the plant, he pointed and explained, warning her the smell of polyester resin would be strong.

While he introduced her to his employees, she couldn't take her eyes off him, though she listened to his enthusiasm about the design of cabin cruisers and runabouts, the history of the business and the process of boatbuilding itself.

Often her attention went to his large hands as they glided over an unfinished hull. The timbre of his voice and the passion in it as he explained what he did, the breadth of his shoulders as he walked beside her glancing over at her, made her feel excited yet protected and safe.

"You have amazing responsibilities here," she noted as they returned to his office a half hour later.

"I guess it seems that way to an outsider, but I grew up here with all of this. Dad and I were partners, so running the business is second nature to me. I'll tell you, Verity, having sole care of Heather daunts me in a way this business never could."

"Why?"

"I guess it goes back to what you said the day we took her to the doctor's. You mentioned you want to teach her what I want her to learn. I knew then you didn't mean the alphabet or arithmetic. Teaching values is a lot more complicated than showing her how to do math. Sometimes I don't know exactly how to go about it," he admitted with a wry turn of his mouth.

"She'll learn values from *you* — from what you say and do and how you treat her."

"Now *that's* responsibility." His blue gaze caught Verity's. They seemed locked together in an intimate understanding when the phone on his desk rang.

Verity murmured, "I should go."

He picked up the receiver, then shook his head. "It's my mother," he explained, holding his hand over the mouthpiece and motioning Verity to the chair in front of his desk. "This won't take long."

Not eager to leave, Verity did as he suggested and perched on the hardwood captain's chair. She had no desire to eavesdrop, and so she cast her gaze around the office as Leo talked, studying a picture next to the TV on the credenza of Leo and an older man who must have been his father, as well as small framed snapshots of Heather. Models of clipper ships also decorated the office file cabinets.

"I know you don't like voice mail, Mom. Calling me here is fine, but if you leave a message on my cell, I *will* call you back."

Whatever his mother said made Leo frown. "You got into town last night?"

Another pause.

"Of course we all want to see you, but it isn't fair to expect Jolene to prepare dinner on such short notice. I'll call her. You can all come to my place and we'll order a pizza." Leo listened for a bit, then replied, "We can order more than one kind. The kids will love it. Come over around seven. Do you want to call Jolene, or should I?"

"All right, I'll take care of it. Are you going to bring your pictures of Hawaii?"

Again there seemed to be another long explanation.

"Jolene and Tim will love a cruise there as a Christmas present. I'll see you around seven."

When Leo hung up, he grinned ruefully. "I always feel as though I've been tossed around in a storm after I've talked to her. We didn't expect her back until a few days before Christmas."

"How long has she been away?"

"Two months. She's leaving again mid-January to visit a friend in England."

"You aren't really going to feed your mother pizza, are you?"

He looked puzzled. "When she jumps in and out of our lives on short notice, it seems the best thing to do."

"I can cook supper."

"You don't have to do that. Jolene and Tim and the kids will be coming over and —"

"I don't mind. Really."

As Leo's steady gaze asked her to give him a further explanation, she went on, "I often miss not having a mother. You shouldn't take yours for granted." That was a bold thing to say, yet she knew Leo always expected honesty from her.

Coming around his desk, he sat on the corner of it. "It's going to be a lot of work."

"It doesn't have to be," she objected. "I can buy tuna steaks at the fresh market and broil them, make a relish for on top, toss a salad, bake a rice pilaf, buy a loaf of French bread. Voilà. Dinner."

"You never cease to amaze me." His low voice made her nerve endings tingle.

"That's because you underestimate me. You think that because I'm a few years younger —"

"Twelve."

"You think that because I'm a few years younger," she repeated, "I haven't had experience at anything. Well, I have, and *not* just with cooking."

As Leo's eyes seemed to linger on her

face then drop to her mouth, he raked his hand through his hair. "Experience aside, you've probably never met anyone like my mother. She isn't always easy to take. She says what she thinks, sometimes without considering the consequences."

"I admire sincerity."

Leo gave a short laugh. "We'll see how long *that* lasts after you meet her." He studied her again. "You're sure you want to take on dinner?"

"Positive."

"All right. But I think it's a good idea if you let Heather stay with Jolene this afternoon. She can bring her along when they come to dinner tonight. That way you can shop and prepare without having to worry about Heather."

"Your daughter isn't a worry, Leo. She's a pleasure."

"Most of the time." He fished his wallet from his back pocket and took out several bills. "Buy whatever you need."

Taking the money, she tucked it into her leather purse. "This is going to be fun."

With a wry smile he stood and returned to his desk chair. "We'll see if you're still wearing rose-colored glasses when the evening is over."

After Verity left Leo's office, she was filled with the anticipation of meeting his mother. No matter what he said, she was going to like her.

Chapter Five

"I hope you're ready for this," Leo said, as he stopped in the kitchen when he got home from work. "Tim and Jolene pulled in behind me in the driveway. Mother's in back of them."

Preparations for the meal had gone well, and Verity felt that she was more than ready. "Dinner will be on the table in fifteen minutes."

After he took a bottle of wine from the refrigerator, Leo peered into the dining room at the vase and the set table. "Did you stop at the florist?"

"No, just at the grocery store. I bought two bunches of flowers and arranged them."

For a few moments he studied the red and white carnations with green filler, the red dinner napkins on the white tablecloth next to the good china that was white with a tiny gray pattern.

Then he remarked, "You should have been a party planner."

His words buoyed Verity because he apparently liked what she had done.

After his observation, he crossed to the counter where she was tossing a salad. She could feel his body heat and smell the scent of his aftershave.

"The corkscrew's in that drawer." He pointed to the area where she was standing, and the look in his eyes lit fires inside of her.

After she moved to the side, he opened the drawer, his hand brushing her hip. As always, she was shaken by the awareness straining between them.

His voice went husky. "I appreciate everything you're doing for tonight."

"Wait and see how it tastes before you tell me that," she joked.

For a second she thought he was going to say something else, but suddenly there was a noisy burst of conversation in the foyer. An instant later Heather ran into the kitchen and wrapped her arms around Verity's legs.

With a smile Verity stooped to give the little girl a hug. "Hi, there. Did you have fun today?"

Heather nodded. "We colowed and went to the playgwound. I swinged."

"That must have been fun."

"Now Randy and Joey came to *my* house to eat." In a sweet rush she added, "We're gonna play some more."

Heather was talking at superfast speed, and Verity could see she was in the souped-up mode that often happened when she was overtired.

"Did you have a nap this afternoon?"

Jolene and the other adults came into the kitchen.

Overhearing the question, Leo's sister answered, "No nap today. Sorry. I tried to put her down for a little while but she didn't want to sleep."

"That happens." Leo scooped up Heather into his arms and carried her over to his mother.

Verity could see at once that Leo didn't resemble his mother. He obviously took after the man she'd seen in the picture in his office at the boatyard. She was striking, though. She wore her white-blond hair in a short, sophisticated cut that angled against her cheeks. Tall — about five-ten — she was also slim. Tonight she'd dressed in beautiful green silk slacks and overshirt.

After Leo made introductions, Amelia Montgomery studied Verity curiously.

Unsure what to wear this evening, Verity had chosen a pair of beige slacks and a no-nonsense, cream oxford shirt. Her brown flat shoes seemed drab compared to

Amelia Montgomery's green high-heeled pumps.

"Leo tells me you're the reason we're not having pizza tonight," his mother said.

"I like to cook," Verity responded easily. "I hope you like tuna."

"Salad?" Amelia asked with a twitch of her nose.

Verity almost laughed at Leo's mother's underestimation of her culinary talents. "No. Broiled tuna steak."

Eyebrows lifting, Amelia asked, "Sushi grade?"

"Of course," Verity answered, trying to keep a straight face.

Amelia's gaze went to the dessert custard sitting on a rack on the counter. "I'm looking forward to a sit-down meal with my family. Thank you for making it possible."

There was more politeness in Amelia's tone than genuine warmth, but Verity didn't let that put her off. She was hoping to get to know Leo's mother. If she did, she might learn more about *him.*

"Let's go wash up," Leo said to Heather.

"I don' wanna wash," she said adamantly, her lower lip quivering.

With Heather pouty, Verity thought, *This might not be the sit-down meal*

Amelia Montgomery expected.

Fifteen minutes later as Verity put the dinner on the table, everyone took their seats except for Heather and five-year-old Joey who were chasing each other around the chairs.

"Whoa!" Leo caught Heather around the waist. "Come on, let's get you settled in your seat."

"No, no, no, Daddy. I don' wanna sit."

On the other side of the table, Jolene was coaxing Joey into his seat.

"Joey's sitting down," Jolene cajoled. "We're going to eat. Aren't you hungry?"

Heather shook her head vigorously. "I'm not hungwy. Don' wanna eat."

Returning to the kitchen for the platter of tuna steak, Verity brought it in, set it in the middle of the table, then took the empty chair next to Jolene.

"You're going to join us?" Amelia asked, not looking as if she quite approved.

Leo, still trying to convince Heather to stay seated, cut a short glance to his mother. "Of course she's going to eat with us. She's not a maid."

Verity knew she should have thought about this. She *didn't* belong here with the family.

When she began to gather her plate and

silverware, Jolene caught her hand. "Uh-uh. You're staying here. Mother, Verity seems to have a quieting effect on the kids. Besides that, we've become friends. She's definitely more than a nanny."

Feeling embarrassed, Verity kept her gaze averted from Leo's because she knew if she didn't, he'd see too much there. She didn't even think of herself as a nanny anymore, and that was dangerous.

While the adults passed the serving dishes, Leo fixed a plate for Heather. But his daughter was definitely cranky, over-tired and petulant. She batted at the dish, spilling the food on the floor.

Verity braced herself for what was coming.

Leo's expression was a study in patience. "If you don't settle down, Heather, you're going to your room. And you can eat when everyone else is finished."

At that, his daughter began to cry, loud wails that seemed to fill the whole house.

Amelia looked pained. Jolene just looked embarrassed. Her husband was enjoying his food as if nothing bothered him. And Jolene had told Verity nothing much did.

Although Leo was firm with Heather, when she cried, he was putty in her hands. He gave Verity one of those looks as if to say, Now what am I supposed to do?

Verity slipped off her chair but didn't go to Heather. Instead she took her own plate which was still empty and quickly arranged some food on it in the shape of a face. Then she took it over to the crying Heather, put her arm around the little girl's shoulders and set the plate before her on the table. "Hey, sweetie. Look what I made for you. Bet you can't eat his nose."

The nose was a grouping of peas.

Suddenly the crying stopped. Heather looked up at Verity, then back at the plate. "It's a *funny* face."

"Well, I guess you could say that. I didn't have a lot to work with. Do you want to eat his nose or his hair?" His hair was made of rice pilaf. Verity handed Heather a spoon.

"I wanna eat his mouf."

Verity had fashioned the mouth from half-cut cherry tomatoes. Hopefully Heather would eventually eat the tuna steak that dotted the face's cheeks. "Okay. You can use your fingers for those."

A few moments later Heather was eating happily and Leo was shaking his head. "I don't know how you do it," he murmured.

"It takes imagination," Jolene offered with a smile. "You use yours for designing boats. Maybe you should take one of those classes Verity's auditing at the college."

Everyone laughed, including Amelia, but as Verity took a clean plate from the hutch and sat beside Jolene again, Leo's mother glanced at her often.

Verity knew Heather would finish her meal much more quickly than everyone else. Since she didn't get involved in the conversation around the table about people she didn't know and places she'd never been, she finished her food about the same time as Heather.

To avoid another scene, when there was a lull in the conversation, Verity asked Leo, "Should I get Heather ready for bed?"

He saw that her plate was empty. "You don't have to do that. I will."

"If you want to spend time with your family, it's okay with me. As soon as she's bored . . ."

His smile was rueful as he nodded. "All right. But come back for dessert."

Not responding to that, Verity rose, gathered Heather into her arms, whispering to her that she could use bubble bath tonight, said good evening to everyone and started for the hall.

She wasn't two steps away from the living room when she heard Amelia's voice and stopped to listen. "She's certainly very capable, but what a plain Jane."

More than once, Verity had heard the old adage that eavesdroppers didn't overhear anything good about themselves, but she couldn't help the tears that sprang to her eyes. Not so much because of Amelia Montgomery's remarks but because she didn't hear the deep rumble of Leo's voice contradicting his mother. She didn't hear anything from him at all.

In the dining room Leo was fuming at what his mother had said about Verity. She *was* very capable, and she *did* dress plainly.

After he took a second helping of tuna and thought about his words carefully, he responded, "Verity is very easy to be around."

His mother looked surprised. "As compared to whom?" she asked promptly.

"As compared to anyone."

"Really? Or were you thinking about Carolyn?"

Maybe he was. Ready for a battle, he laid down his fork. His mother had adored Carolyn, constantly reminding him that his wife was perfect for him. "Maybe I *am* making a comparison. It's easier to be around a low-maintenance woman than a high-maintenance one."

Carolyn had definitely been high maintenance, just like his mother. Her hair had to always be perfectly in place, as did her makeup and her clothes. If she didn't have a manicure every week, she was embarrassed to go out.

"I'm not exactly sure what you mean by high maintenance," his mother replied haughtily, "but a little makeup never hurt anyone. Verity's basically a beautiful girl. She just doesn't know it. No one around her does, either. Contact lenses would make a world of difference."

"Mom, you can't change everyone you meet," Jolene admonished.

"Whom have I tried to change?"

"All of us," Jolene answered lightly. "You want Leo to dress in a suit and go to work every day as if he works on Wall Street. Even though he has an MBA, he works in a *boatyard.* And me. You think I should get out and go to book-discussion groups and join the bridge club when I enjoy spending time at home cooking and gardening more."

Amelia glanced over at Tim speculatively. "Do you have any complaints?"

"Not a one," he responded blandly, and

Leo watched Jolene smile. That's what Jolene loved about her husband. He never got into an argument if he could help it.

"Look, Mom. Verity's doing a wonderful job with Heather. That's all that matters to me," Leo said.

"Is it?" his mother asked, as if she knew that every time he looked at Verity his blood pressure went up.

She couldn't know that. Could she?

When his gaze fell on Jolene, his sister shrugged her shoulders. "I can't wait to try that cream custard Verity made for dessert. Why don't I go put on a pot of coffee?"

Instead of sitting here having coffee and dessert with his family, Leo realized he'd rather be putting Heather to bed alongside Verity. That thought shook up his world, as did his mother's knowing glances as he finished dinner.

After his family left, Leo went to Heather's room. She was sleeping peacefully, Nosy tucked in by her side. She'd had an active day and with no nap, she'd probably sleep late in the morning. Not sure what prodded him, he went to the kitchen, spooned portions of the leftover custard Verity had made into two dishes and took them along with him to Verity's room. Her door was slightly ajar.

When he looked inside, he saw her lying on her sofa, a book on her lap. She was sleeping.

Studying her in sleep, he realized how very pretty she was. Her long ponytail lay over her shoulder, and he longed to unband it and run his fingers through her glossy hair. Not wanting to startle her, feeling like an intruder in her room, juggling the two dishes in one hand, he rapped on her door.

Instantly alert, she swung her legs to the floor and sat up. "Leo!"

Taking her exclamation as an invitation to come in, he crossed the room and sat on the sofa next to her, placing the custards on the coffee table. "Hi. I think the family exhausted you."

"I wasn't really sleeping. I just sort of dozed off."

He laughed. "You were sleeping. After caring for a three-year-old, making dinner for company and cleaning up, I can see why. I brought you dessert."

Glancing away from him, she focused on the custard. "Thanks."

"Why didn't you rejoin us in the great room after you put Heather to bed?"

"I didn't want to intrude."

Verity had brought something into his life that had been missing — peace, sunshine, energy that made him feel alive again.

"I told you my mother was hard to take sometimes."

A shadow crossed Verity's face. "She's just looking out for you. For all of you," she amended.

"She knows better than to think she has to look out for me."

"Heather, then. She wants to make sure any influence in her life is a good one."

"You're the best. She couldn't have anyone better looking after her." He wasn't just trying to reassure Verity. He meant it.

Apparently she could see that, and her eyes suddenly glistened. "Thank you, Leo. That's nice of you to say."

Sometimes he got the feeling that Verity didn't know her own worth. Cupping her cheek, he said gently, "That wasn't just an idle compliment. You're good for Heather." Honestly he added, "And you're good for me."

When her eyes widened, when her lips parted slightly, he couldn't help leaning into her. He couldn't help putting his arm around her. He couldn't help kissing her. Verity Sumpter brightened his world and drew him like a magnet. He still wasn't altogether sure why, but she aroused him in a way he'd never been aroused before. It definitely wasn't just physical, though that was a big part of it.

As Leo's lips angled over Verity's, he realized all the things he felt when he was with her. He felt taller, stronger, more of a man, as if he was capable of holding the world on his shoulders. He felt as if he could be a success at raising Heather. He felt his ties to Jolene more keenly, and even appreciated his mother a little more.

Why was all of that so?

Kissing Verity, he tried to find the answer. But as his tongue slipped into her mouth, as she caught her breath and then responded to him, he got lost in everything physical. When Verity wrapped her arms around his neck, when he felt her soft breasts against his chest, when he tasted her sweetness, and experienced arousal that was almost painful, nothing but the physical mattered. She seemed as lost to the chemistry between them as he was, as her hands slid into his hair.

After he broke their kiss to nuzzle her neck, he touched his tongue to the pulse at her throat, and she murmured his name. It was a sexy whisper that was as erotic as everything else they were doing. He brought one of his hands between them and pressed his palm to her breast. When she moaned, he did it again. Kissing her once more, he passed his thumb over her nipple. It was a hard bud, and he could feel it through her blouse . . . through her bra. Her tongue played with his and he teased the nipple, taunted it, made her want more. He could tell she did. As her tongue stroked his, as her hands slipped from his hair down his neck to his shoulders, as she curled her fingers into his muscles, he pictured her hands on his bare skin and thought about how he would feel. He hadn't been touched by a woman in so very long.

Without thinking about repercussions, only thinking about hunger and need, his fingers went to the buttons on her blouse. He started unfastening them rapidly, fumbling when one wouldn't come loose, all the while getting hotter because of Verity's willing responses, the soft sounds she made, her hand exploring what she could reach. Finally he slipped his hand inside her blouse. Her bra was silky, lace edging the cup. He dipped his thumb inside —

Verity froze. Absolutely froze. Her stillness was a sharp contrast to the playfulness of her tongue and the exploration of her fingers a moment before.

Breathing raggedly, he broke away and gazed down at her. "What's wrong?"

Her eyes were huge, velvety, and so vulnerable. She said, "I have to tell you something."

"Now?" he asked, lightly teasing.

When she nodded, her expression was completely serious. "I . . . I'm a virgin."

Leo wasn't sure whether to be shocked, amazed or totally baffled. "A virgin? You've been to college. You've dated."

"Matthew was my first serious relationship. He wanted to, but I . . ." She scooted her gaze from his. "I wasn't ready. It's another reason he . . . moved on."

So many thoughts battled for dominance in Leo all at once. "If he couldn't wait until you were ready, then he didn't love you."

At that, her eyes came up to meet his. "That's what Sean said. I thought he was just being a brother."

"He was being a man, too. A man who knows how other guys should treat women." Leo raked his hand through his hair and moved away from her, as much from his own need to cool down as from what she'd told him.

"Leo, I . . . liked what we were doing. I just thought you should know."

"Now I know. Why have you waited?" he asked, needing to hear the answer.

"I was waiting for the right man . . . the man I wanted to spend my life with. I know that might seem silly. Maybe I should have been born a few decades earlier. But I just can't imagine being intimate with a man without knowing we have a commitment to each other and that being together is right."

"There's nothing silly at all about believing that," he said gruffly. "But I'm glad you told me because I'm not at all sure about the rightness of this. I don't think *you* are, either. We just got caught up in the moment."

"But . . ."

"No buts, Verity. I won't take advantage of you. You were sleeping when I came in here. I shouldn't have let this attraction between us get out of hand."

"I was awake when you kissed me. I was awake when *I* kissed *you*. You seem to think because I'm younger than you I don't know up from down, left from right, or the consequences of what I do. Believe me, Leo, I understand consequences. I understand exactly what was happening between us."

He was going to see how really honest she was. "Were you ready for it?"

With a shaky smile, she answered, "I don't know. But I didn't want you to stop."

"On some level, you did. That's why you told me you were a virgin."

"No. I just thought you should know."

"You stopped me instinctively, and that was the right thing to do. The right thing for *me* to do now is leave."

After a moment she suggested, "We *could* eat dessert together."

"We could. But I think it's wiser for me to get a cold shower."

When she blushed, he felt every one of those twelve years that gave him so much more experience than she'd ever had. "I just wanted to apologize for my mother in case she made you feel uncomfortable tonight."

Still for a few seconds, Verity finally said, "Your mother put the situation in perspective for me. I'm not one of the family, Leo. You pay me to take care of Heather."

Yes, he did, and before he muddied the waters, he'd better make sure he was putting Heather's interests first. Letting Verity's statement stand, he told her, "I have an early meeting in the morning. I'll be leaving the house before Heather gets up."

"But you'll be home for supper?"

"Yes. Even though you're excellent with Heather, I want to make sure she knows I'm always going to be around, that she comes first in my life, and that she matters to me."

After he crossed to the door, he stopped. "Thanks again for putting dinner together tonight. I won't forget it."

With Verity's soft "Good night" ringing in his ears he headed for his bedroom, knowing he wouldn't forget her response to his kisses or his response to her touch, either.

He didn't just need a cold shower. He needed a *long,* cold shower.

Rain drizzled down the following day when Leo came home from work and saw the letters shoved in the mailbox on the porch. Apparently Verity had been too busy with Heather to even come outside for the mail. Carrying it into the foyer, he sorted through it on the table and found a letter for Verity. In the upper lefthand corner was simply the name Will, instead of a return address.

Curious, yet knowing he had no right to question her about it, he strode into the kitchen where she was making dinner.

Heather was standing on a chair next to Verity at the counter, watching her stir batter for biscuits.

After he kissed and hugged his daughter, he said nonchalantly to Verity, "You have a letter." He held it up to her so she could see the front of the envelope.

She smiled. It was a quirky little smile that made him wonder if it had come from the guy she'd spoken to at the arts festival. After all, she was young and pretty, and probably had lots of boys who wanted to date her. Boys. Leo was definitely a man. His thoughts about her were anything but pure, especially in his dreams.

Without giving any hints as to what the letter might contain, she simply asked, "Would you mind putting it on my desk in my sitting room? I don't want to lose it."

If she didn't want to lose it, that meant the letter was important.

Suddenly he found himself wanting to know where she went on her Sundays off. He wanted to know more about her, and there was only one way to do that — spend some time with her.

Still fingering the letter, an idea came to him, and he ran with it. "How would you like to do something a little different to-morrow?"

"Like what?"

"Every year, weather permitting, I have a party for my employees on the beach for Christmas. For years they've been telling me they enjoy that more than some dinner-dance in a hotel. It'll start about four and last into the evening. Would you like to go? The weather report for tomorrow sounds promising."

She looked a little puzzled, as if she wondered if he were asking her on a date. Damned if he knew!

"Heather, too?"

"Oh, no. This is strictly for adults. I'm going to take Jolene's boys Christmas shopping after school one day next week so I don't think she'll mind watching Heather. My mom will have a chance to spend some time with her, too."

"Then I'd like to come to your beach party." Verity's eyes sparkled, as if a jaunt to the beach was exactly what she'd like to do.

He found himself looking forward to it, too. "Dress casually. Nothing fancy. Do you play beach volleyball?" he asked.

With a wide grin, she nodded. "Absolutely."

"Great. The employees have the afternoon off. I'll come home and pick you up and grab the volleyball gear."

The letter still feeling like a hot potato in his hand, he moved a little closer to Verity and peered over her shoulder at the batter. "I don't know if I've ever had homemade biscuits."

"Not even as a kid?"

"Mom wasn't very domestic." His lips were tantalizingly near her cheek. Her hair smelled fragrant . . . of spices and flowers. "What are we having with them?" he asked, his voice low.

She kept stirring. "Chili. If you like it hot I'll add more peppers."

"I like it hot."

She turned then, her skin grazing his, her gaze meeting his. "I'll remember that," she murmured.

"Daddy, Daddy. I'm gonna eat chili and biscuits, too."

Leo grinned. He realized that Heather heard a lot more than he'd thought she did. She was looking up at him as he stood so very close to Verity, and he almost felt as if they were a family.

That thought was a shock.

Moving away from Verity, he ruffled his daughter's hair. "I think we'll make some chili for you that isn't quite so hot."

Then he tickled his daughter and went

to Verity's sitting room to deposit her letter on her desk. Already he was thinking about tomorrow and playing volleyball with Verity. He just wanted to spend more time with her . . . get to know her a little better.

In a flash of memory, he recalled Carolyn's first outing on the beach with his employees as well as her decision not to attend in the years after that. She simply hadn't been a sand-between-her-toes kind of person. He had a suspicion Verity was.

Realizing that, he knew he might have bitten off a lot more than he could chew.

Chapter Six

Waves sloshed on the beach as the sun dipped into the gold-and-pink horizon. Adjusting the elastic band she'd brought along to hold her glasses in place, Verity readied herself for the volleyball game.

She didn't feel as if she belonged here.

Although everyone was friendly, Leo was the one who was giving her that impression. Once they'd arrived, he'd become engaged in one conversation after another, leaving her on her own. Not that she minded that. She enjoyed going from group to group, getting to know people. But he was giving the impression he'd just brought her along for a game of volleyball. Maybe that's exactly what he'd done. Maybe she'd read more into this invitation than she should have.

So if he'd brought her along to play volleyball, that was what she was going to do. She was wearing purple running pants and a matching shirt she'd bought a while back and never worn. Volleyball was her game. She'd been on a team in high school, and she hadn't forgotten the moves.

She slipped into place on the side opposite of Leo. However, they had a shortage of players. The other side had an abundance, and Leo jogged over to stand behind her. She tried not to notice him in his cutoff shorts and a red T-shirt that stretched over his muscles like a second skin. She tried to ignore his hair blowing in the breeze and the strong cut of his jaw, as well as his powerful physique.

Staring straight ahead, she was determined to concentrate on the game.

Play began with a soaring high serve, and Verity was ready. The ball came straight to her, and she whacked it over the net. As the game grew fast and furious, she thought she'd forget about Leo behind her. But she didn't. She only knew she had to make every shot she could.

Verity was surprised that Leo was as expert at playing volleyball as she was and made it look effortless. When she swiveled to watch him take a shot, she marveled at everything about his tall, hard body.

As the sky turned purple with dusk, the ball became harder to see. They'd soon have to call it quits and were trying to get in as many shots as they could. When the ball sailed toward Verity again, she had to take a few back-up steps.

Suddenly there was a thwump as she and Leo collided, reaching for the same hit. The ball glanced off her shoulder and bounced away, but Leo's arms went around her to steady her. He was hot, male, sweaty, and she could feel the rise and fall of his chest at her shoulder. His arms were tight around her, and she knew she never wanted him to let her go. What a silly thought in the middle of a volleyball game!

He turned her around in his arms and steadied her. "Are you okay?"

She was fine, except she couldn't breathe very well. "Just had some air knocked out of me," she answered breathlessly, more from the contact with Leo and the hungry glimmers of desire in his eyes than from their collision.

"I thought it was too far back for you."

"I thought I could reach it," she murmured inanely, her pulse racing, every nerve in her body rioting.

As the waxing moon glowed down upon them, the shadows didn't seem so thick. Leo's face was so close to hers, she could almost brush her lips against his jaw.

Someone cleared his throat and a male voice asked, "Leo?"

Leo tore his gaze from hers and looked over his shoulder.

"It's getting pretty dark. Maybe we should quit." The man who said it was in his thirties, had short-cropped brown hair, and was trying to hide a smile.

His gaze went to Verity, and it was appreciative, as it passed over her clinging top and knit pants. "You did a perfect job. You can be on *my* team anytime. I don't think I caught your name."

"It's Verity. Verity Sumpter."

"And you're a friend of Leo's?" The man was waiting for some type of clarification.

"Verity came with me," Leo responded a bit possessively.

"I see," the man commented with a frown. Then he smiled again at Verity and extended his hand. "The name's Jim Ross. It's good to meet you. Are you ready for the bonfire?"

"Bonfire?" Verity asked.

"Yep. It's a tradition. I guess Leo didn't tell you. We sit around it and cook hotdogs, eat marshmallows. There are coolers over there filled with side dishes, too." He winked at her. "The boss bought it all, so eat as much as you want."

Leo hadn't told her much about what was happening tonight. The bonfire sounded nice, yet she still felt uncomfortable and out of place.

The rest of the volleyball teams had broken up and the players were scattering toward the fire that had been started along the beach. Jim said to Leo, "I brought my guitar and so did Dave."

Leo gave him a forced smile. "That's great. We'll have entertainment after we eat."

"It takes everyone a while, but eventually they'll warm up to a sing-along," Jim told her. "I'll expect you to join in."

Verity nodded, and with a last look, Jim Ross walked away.

She and Leo were left on the sand under the moon. But only for a moment.

Someone called from the group gathering around the fire. "Hey, Leo. We have everything all set up. Come and get it."

"I have to stay for the bonfire," he told Verity. "But if you want to leave after we eat, we can."

"That's fine." She thought he just wanted to take her home because this was an awkward situation for him. Perhaps he was sorry he'd asked her along.

A short while later, Leo made sure everyone had enough food. As he headed toward the bonfire and took a seat in the circle around it next to Verity, he realized she fit in here better than Carolyn ever had. Verity had truly enjoyed that game of volleyball. She had a competitive edge and it showed. She also had a way with people.

He remembered the way Jim Ross had looked at Verity. A feeling so foreign had gripped Leo he hadn't recognized it right away. He'd felt a hint of it at the arts festival when Verity's classmate had approached her. Finally he labeled it — jealousy. Leo couldn't remember ever being jealous of Carolyn or feeling possessive. Although she'd been beautiful, a layer of reserve had kept other men from coming too close . . . had kept Leo from getting too close. Verity didn't have any of that reserve. She was genuine and friendly and approachable.

As Leo's shoulder brushed Verity's, he turned over the campfire appliance that roasted four hot dogs at once. The meat sizzled, smoked aroma filling the air along with the bonfire and the sea. When Leo glanced at Verity, she had her knees pulled up before her, her arms around them, and she was staring into the fire.

The tension between them was his fault, but it seemed safer than attraction. He'd been remiss in not introducing her properly to his employees. Truth be told, he hadn't known what to say. She wasn't his date, exactly. Yet he didn't want to simply introduce her as Heather's nanny. The lack of acknowledgment on his part had made her feel awkward, and he was sorry about that. With everyone sitting around, talking, listening to each other's conversations, this wasn't the place to tell her.

They'd eaten, and Jim and Dave were strumming a rendition of "Deck the Halls," when Dave's wife asked Leo, "What are you getting for Heather this Christmas?"

"I haven't gone shopping yet," Leo admitted.

"You mean she hasn't asked for everything she sees on TV?"

"We don't let her watch that much TV, so I think she'll be happy with almost anything Santa Claus brings."

"There's a new educational store for kids over on Yellow Rose Boulevard," one of the other wives mentioned. "I spent over an hour there. You might want to check it out."

Leo leaned close to Verity. "Maybe I could get home early some afternoon and we could stop in."

"Or maybe you and Jolene should check it out," Verity said quietly.

Leo had asked Verity along today because he thought she'd have fun. However, now he saw that he'd simply put her in an awkward situation. He hadn't meant to do that, and now he realized he had to take a stand where Verity was concerned. The silvery moon shone brightly on the water. They wouldn't need a flashlight if they went for a walk on the beach.

Leaning close to her he suggested, "Come for a walk with me."

She glanced at him, her eyes puzzled.

As he stood, he offered her his hand. When she took it, he tugged her up.

At the edge of the circle, he slipped off his deck shoes. Seeing what he had done, she slipped off her sneakers and socks, then rolled up her pants. Before Leo could even think about what came next, she was running across the sand to the packed part of the beach, letting the water catch her toes and slosh around her. He found himself doing the same thing, snatching her hand and running down the beach with her. He felt freer than he'd felt in years. Verity did that. She loosened something that had become coiled much too tightly inside of him.

When they stopped running and caught their breath, she stooped to pick up a shell and examined it in the moonlight.

Leo found himself clasping her shoulder and turning her to him. "I never meant for you to feel out of place tonight."

"I'm fine, Leo."

"Maybe. Or maybe you're just too polite to say what you're thinking."

She shook her head. "I'm not thinking anything. I'm just trying to live in the moment."

He wondered if she did that because of losing her twin . . . if now she realized how very precious every moment was. He was beginning to realize that, too. "Once we got here tonight I didn't know how to explain you. I haven't been out in public with a woman since I lost my wife."

She took that in. "You haven't dated?"

"Nope. So tonight, when I brought you along and we got a few stares, I decided to skip over introductions. That wasn't fair to you."

Turning away from him, she stared out into the ocean and then looked up at the sky, as if she expected to see something specific. Finally she said, "It's okay, Leo."

"No, it's not." Taking her hand, he tugged her a little closer. "I have to climb off the fence where you're concerned. It's just . . . you're *so* young."

"You've got a hangup about that," she remarked, so seriously he had to smile.

"I guess I do. But I can tell you why. You're unlike any other woman I've ever been attracted to. You make me see the world differently. Colors seem brighter. The days seem fuller. I appreciate every-thing Heather does in a way I didn't be-fore. I was growing more distant from her, and you brought me back."

"You would have found your way back."

Leo traced her cheekbones with his thumbs and turned her face up to his. "I don't know what it is about you, Verity, but I can't seem to stay away from you. You've got your whole life ahead of you."

"So do you," she suggested gently.

After Carolyn died, his path had been clear — to work hard to make a future for his daughter. It had been a road without any turnoffs, a road without any forks to make it interesting. Verity had become a fork in the road, and he wasn't sure whether he should take it, for her sake as well as his.

Trembling all over, Verity felt as if she and Leo were perched on a precipice. One false step and they'd fall. She wasn't too young for him, but she might be too inex-perienced. As unsure as Leo was about them, she was that unsure, too. Could she trust what was happening between them? Could she trust that it was serious to him? Could she believe she was more than a distraction until he found the woman of his dreams? She was so afraid that once she offered him her heart he'd walk away. She was so afraid that the feelings she had for him were so much deeper than the ones he had for her.

She knew it was silly, but she wished, somehow, Sean could give her a sign. They'd always told each other when they were apart and they saw a shooting star, that star would be a message from one to the other. Because of their twin connection, they'd read the message and know what the star meant. She wished for a shooting star now. She wished Sean was here to give her advice. She wished so many things.

Her wishes took wings as Leo became her only focus. They lifted and scattered and flew as his arms went around her . . . as she breathed in his scent . . . as she tipped her chin up to accept his kiss. Tonight's kiss was different from the others. It was hungrier. It was demanding. It was possessive. The pressure of his lips, the sweep of his tongue, the tautness of his body told her he was letting go of more of his restraint. He was letting himself feel the chemistry between them, and he was going with it.

Far away, she heard the strains of a Christmas carol, voices blending with the guitars, a sea horn blaring out in the Gulf. The scents of saltwater and damp sand and Leo's aftershave combined, until she knew she'd remember the mix forever. The sand was cold now between her toes, and it was a sharp contrast to the heat she was feeling in her body.

Leo's hand passed up and down her back, pressing her closer, until she could feel his arousal as keenly as she could feel her own.

Seconds later, however, he loosened his hold and stepped away. "We've got to slow this down."

She knew he was right, but not being in his arms didn't feel right, either.

"We both need time to think about what we want," he said, almost to himself.

"Sometimes thinking will get you into as much trouble as doing."

He blew out a breath, shook his head and smiled at her. "Where did those words of wisdom come from?"

Laughing, she admitted, "I don't remember. But they sounded good, don't you think?"

Still smiling, he wrapped an arm around her shoulders. "What I think is that we should get back before someone sends out a search party. Besides, we need to practice harmonizing on Christmas carols so we can do it with Heather. I'll stop for a tree tomorrow, and then we'll see if we can really usher in the holidays."

For the past month Verity had dreaded the idea of the holidays without Sean. Now she was looking forward to them. Leo and Heather were filling her life in a way she never expected.

Studying the sky, she hoped to see a shooting star. But only every-night stars twinkled back. However, as Leo took her hand in his, she forgot about heavenly bodies and welcomed the warm, tingling feelings holding his hand gave her.

When Leo brought the tree in Saturday afternoon, Heather was napping.

"Good," he commented when Verity told him. "This tree will be a lot easier to put up without little hands and feet in the way. What's that great smell?"

"Heather and I made gingerbread men for the tree."

Leo straightened the evergreen in the stand. "Is this going to be an old-fashioned tree with popcorn strings, too?"

"I thought that might be fun. Heather might like to make a few ornaments to hang, too."

Their gazes connected and held, and Verity could see Leo liked her suggestion. After they'd come home last night, he hadn't kissed her again, but when they'd said good night she'd seen the same hunger in his eyes that she'd seen on the beach. They were headed someplace exciting. She was scared and thrilled all at the same time.

Tearing his gaze from hers, Leo held the tree and tightened the bolts holding it in place on the stand. Then he angled a few feet away and studied it. "That's as straight as it's going to get. I have lights and ornaments in the attic. I'll go get them."

"Need help?" Verity asked.

"Not for this. I'll need your help when Heather wants to poke into every box and plug in every light." Then he went to the spare bedroom where there was a trap door and stairs that pulled down from the attic space.

Verity prepared and stuffed a chicken to roast in the oven for supper. By the time she'd done that, she realized Leo still hadn't returned with any boxes. Curious, suspecting the Christmas lights were tangled and he was trying to unravel them, she put one of the cooled gingerbread men on a napkin for Leo and carried it down the hall. Peeking into Heather's room, she saw the little girl was still sleeping.

The door to the guest bedroom was open and Verity went in. This room was pleasantly decorated in green and wine. The pine bedroom suite was substantial and the bed wore a geometrically designed coverlet. Stairs that had been pulled down from the attic hooked Verity's attention.

Crossing to them, she started up. When she reached the top step, she took in the area with a glance. There wasn't much stored there — a few boxes, a set of luggage, baby paraphernalia that Heather had outgrown already. Leo had found the lights. They were sitting in a neat coil at his feet. He was seated beside a cardboard ornament box and she could see he held a white-and-gold one in his hand.

"That's beautiful."

"Every ornament in this box is almost too delicate to touch."

Looking down at the opened box, she

saw fragile, blown-glass ornaments as well as hand-painted ones.

"We had an artificial tree," Leo explained, pointing to a tall box in the corner.

Suddenly Verity understood that memories of Christmases past had grabbed Leo and that his ties to his wife might never be broken. She understood those emotions. Yet, seeing Leo like this with the ornaments hurt her because his reaction meant he wasn't ready for a new involvement.

Walking over to him, she crouched down beside him. "Do you want me to take the box downstairs? I'll be careful."

He looked at the gingerbread cookie in her hand and then back at the ornaments. "No, I don't think we can use them. I wouldn't want any of them to break. I'll keep them for when Heather's older. When she's not as likely to go over to the tree, pluck one off and toss it like a ball." His half smile was meant to tell her everything was fine, and she shouldn't be concerned about him or the ornaments.

She felt foolish standing there holding the cookie. "I brought this up in case you wanted to taste one."

Taking it from her he said, "Thanks. I'll be down in a minute."

It would take more than a minute for Leo to sort through his memories.

When Verity descended the attic steps, Heather was standing at the bottom, Nosy tucked under her arm. "*Me* want to see what's up there."

Heather's big bed was supposed to arrive on Monday. They'd ordered it so they wouldn't have to worry about her falling if she crawled out of her crib. Apparently she'd mastered the skill!

Crouching down to the little girl, Verity put her arm around her. "I'll bet there's something you'd rather see in the great room." She took her hand. "Daddy brought it in. Come on, I'll show you."

The idea of something exciting in the great room tantalized Heather. She only gave one more look over her shoulder before she let Verity lead her away.

True to his word, Leo joined them a few minutes later. Heather was still looking up at the tree with awe.

"We have to ice the gingerbread men," Verity explained to the three-year-old. "We can hang them on the branches. We can make other ornaments to hang with ribbon, too. Do you want to do that?"

Heather looked intrigued by the whole idea, nodded vigorously, then ran to the kitchen to get started.

"This is going to be messy," Verity said with a smile, trying to gauge Leo's mood.

"Anything concerning Heather and food is messy." He'd carried down a carton with coils of lights lying on top. "I'll work on the lights while you and Heather make ornaments."

She wasn't sure how to act with him, whether or not they should go into this Christmas full force for Heather's sake, or to tread lightly for his.

He must have read her concern. "I'll find CDs of Christmas carols. Heather will like them."

How about you? she wanted to ask . . . but didn't.

A half hour later, Heather had lost interest in icing the cookies, and Verity was just waiting for a few more to harden for the tree. The three-year-old had migrated to the small table and chairs where she'd arranged a doll and two teddy bears to watch her while she colored.

When Leo came into the kitchen, he took in the scene in a glance. "The tree has lights. Now we just need everything else."

"I'll be finished here in a minute. Then we can start stringing. This decorating process could take a few days."

Leo's somber mood seemed to have slid away. Or else he was hiding it well. "That will give Heather something to do."

Verity laughed and playfully dipped her finger into the bowl, then held it up for Leo. "Want a taste?"

There was no hesitation in him as he leaned forward and caught her finger between his lips. The sensation was so sensual she felt her knees wobble. She thought they would buckle altogether when his tongue laved her skin. The flare of desire in his eyes mesmerized her, and she couldn't look away.

Sensually, his lips slowly released her finger. She felt as if he'd touched her intimately. The smoldering heat in his eyes told her he was thinking of things other than cookies and icing and his daughter as he slipped his hand beneath her hair. "It's a shame Heather still isn't napping."

"Maybe it's not," she said quietly, realizing why Leo might be touching her now. "Maybe I want to be more than a distraction from your memories."

His expression changed. The smoldering desire became anger as his shoulders straightened and he crossed his arms over his chest. "Is that what you believe, Verity? Or are you just afraid to take the next step, and my history's a convenient excuse not to?"

Without waiting for an answer he strode across the kitchen, hunkered down beside Heather and asked, "Are you ready to decorate the tree?"

Verity knew she had probably just put another wedge between them, but if he wanted her to be honest, she couldn't hide her thoughts. Sure, her inexperience and fear might be part of the mix. She'd overcome fear before. What she couldn't overcome were Leo's ties to his past.

Could she?

Chapter Seven

When Leo returned home from taking Jolene's boys Christmas shopping, he strode down the hall to Heather's room, wondering what Verity's mood would be. He had to admit he'd been angry with her Saturday night. Because she'd told him the truth?

His excursion into the attic had awakened sleeping memories. He was discovering that his marriage hadn't been all that he'd wanted it to be. So when he'd walked into the kitchen, seen Verity icing cookies, Heather playing so contentedly nearby, the tableau had created in him an unfamiliar yearning. Instead of dealing with that yearning and where it was coming from, he'd latched on to something easy — the desire Verity awakened without even trying.

Something about Verity got to him in such an elemental way, his usual ironclad restraint let loose. Yesterday had been her day off and all day he'd wondered how she was spending it . . . where she'd gone . . . if she was with another man. Her classmate, maybe? After she'd returned home in the evening, she'd looked in on Heather, then disappeared into her rooms.

Now as he came to the door of Heather's room, he stopped abruptly. Everything had changed inside of it. The furniture had been delivered, and it looked like a little girl's haven. He realized that didn't have as much to do with the furniture as what Verity had done with it.

"If you don't like it, I can take the spread and curtains back," Verity said from the bed where she was sitting next to Heather, a book across their laps.

The white wood bed with its turned spool design on the headboard, dresser and chest was elegantly feminine. He'd chosen this suite because Heather could grow into it, and the furniture would fit her even as an adult. However, beyond that, what someone had done to the room was charming. The quilted spread and matching curtains were printed with favorite nursery rhymes. On the wall hung a cloth tapestry of a cow jumping over the moon. There were pink scarves on the chest and dresser as well as a light with a pink-polka-dot lampshade.

"The room looked so barren," Verity explained. "I'd seen this set at the department store. But if you don't like it, I can pack it all up —"

Leo wasn't exactly sure what he felt about it. On one hand, he knew Carolyn would have hired a decorator to take care of the room. On the other, he felt as if Verity knew Heather better than he did. He wouldn't have known where to start. She had a mother's instincts where his daughter was concerned, and that seemed to bother him most of all because of the repercussions the fact carried with it.

"I think it's just right," he admitted. "How did you pay for it?"

"I had some money put aside for Christmas. I knew if you liked it you'd reimburse me. If you don't like it, I could return it for a refund. I probably should have called you and asked first, but things were kind of tense between us, and I didn't want to interrupt you at work."

Again, that truth that Verity seemed to have no trouble stating.

"You could have called. I'd put aside anything between us to consider Heather."

Apparently tired of waiting, Heather tugged on Verity's arm. "Can we wead the stowy now?"

Verity's gaze lifted to his, as if she were asking him if he wanted to read the book to his daughter. He did. "Hey, kiddo. How about if I read it to you?"

Heather looked from one of them to the other, then gave a little shrug. "Okay."

Verity gave Heather a hug and whispered, "Sweet dreams." Then, with a last look at Leo, she left the room.

He wished he knew what was going through her head. He wished he could control the attraction he felt for her. He wished he didn't feel in such turmoil about all of it.

After Leo tucked in his daughter, he went to the pool house. Losing himself in work had always helped him solve problems . . . or had insulated him from them. The night was cool so he lit a fire in the fireplace and settled himself at the drafting board. After he wrote a check for everything Verity had purchased and set it aside, he turned to his work. Nevertheless, the new design didn't call to him as it had yesterday. Still, he picked up his pencil and started making adjustments.

The fire licked at the logs as he became absorbed in his work. He wasn't sure how much time had passed when there was a knock at the pool house door. The baby monitor was quiet, so he knew Verity's visit didn't have anything to do with his daughter. He motioned her to come in.

After she opened the door and stepped inside, she smiled unsurely. "There's something I need to talk to you about."

Rising from his stool, he motioned to the sofa. It was tan leather and comfortable, as was everything else in here. He'd found a local artist to paint a lighthouse mural on one wall. Other than that, the space was simply furnished and the refuge he wanted it to be.

The thought suddenly hit him that he'd needed a refuge from Carolyn, the lifestyle she'd wanted, the pastimes she'd chosen. He'd have to dissect that later.

Perched on the edge of his couch, Verity looked as if she were going to fly away any moment. He suddenly realized how much he wanted her to stay. "What did you need to talk to me about?" He sat beside her with about six inches separating them, but he was angled toward her and could already feel the sparks.

"Heather's teacher called this morning. The school's having a Christmas program on Thursday."

"I know. I have it on my calendar. I can take her that day and give you a break."

"That's what her teacher wanted to talk to me about. Apparently, Heather assumes we'll both be there. Since her teacher's taking a head count, she wanted to make sure. If Heather wants me there, I'd love to go, but I didn't know how you'd feel about that."

He studied the nanny Heather had obviously become so attached to. As always, Verity had tied her hair back in a ponytail. Her skin was beautifully perfect with a healthy, peachy glow now that made his fingers itch to touch it. She wore jeans and a sweater that came practically to her knees.

But he knew what was underneath. He'd felt it when they'd pressed together. She was curvy and feminine, and the nondescript clothes were a tease in their own way. When he studied her serious expression, he realized she obviously didn't want to overstep any boundaries and found that aspect of her character totally endearing.

"Of course you should go to the Christmas program. Apparently, Heather will be disappointed if you're not there."

He still saw concern on Verity's face, then knew instinctively what was causing it. "You're thinking it will be moms and dads and you might feel out of place?"

"Not exactly that, but I don't want anyone to mistake me for someone I'm not."

She didn't have to say more than that. He was taken back to the night when Tony Parelli had arrived and jumped to conclusions. "It doesn't matter what anybody else thinks. If someone gets it wrong, we'll correct them. Jolene has been around, but Heather has never had a constant woman's presence before. I'm grateful for you, Verity. You've made a difference here. And you need to know that Saturday, in the kitchen, you were much more than a distraction."

After staring into the fire crackling in the hearth, she finally returned her gaze to his. "You accused me of being afraid. I am. I've never felt anything as strong as the chemistry between us."

He hadn't, either. Taking her face between his palms, he said huskily, "I don't want you to be afraid. But we need to take this slowly for both our sakes."

As he touched her, every cell in his body shouted at him to do a hell of a lot more. He actually ached to feel her under him . . . to join their bodies . . . to end this craving that was interfering with his life.

With their gazes locked together now, Verity's hands slid into the thickness of his hair.

"Verity," he breathed, leaning closer,

tamping down primitive urges.

He kissed her forehead, the tip of her cute nose, and then his mouth was on hers, opening, eager to teach her everything she'd never learned. He'd kept his feelings in check, but now he couldn't deny his desire. As the kiss grew more incendiary, as their tongues played and mated, as he could feel her response down to his boots, he wanted more. Sliding his hands from her face to her shoulders, he stroked her arms. She strained toward him, and he was experiencing the same restless urgency. Still, he was aware that Verity was a virgin, and he didn't want to rush anything. He also knew he was going to have to stop.

But not now. Not yet.

Finally breaking the kiss minutes later, he murmured, "Have you ever been touched by a man?"

Her cheeks became red. "Matthew groped a little, but —"

He couldn't help but smile. "If at any time you feel I'm groping, you say so."

Her shy smile and her tiny nod filled him with the desire to take her in his arms once more. Kissing her again, he tugged her sweater up over her hips, but he didn't lift it over her head. He had a feeling Verity would be much too self-conscious naked.

Instead, he slipped his hand beneath her sweater and let it rest on her midriff. He felt her shiver.

"Are you okay?" he asked.

She nodded. "Very okay. Can I touch *you?*" she asked.

"Be my guest," he answered gruffly, never more aroused.

"I want to touch your skin," she whispered into his neck.

He laughed and tugged his knit shirt from his jeans, then lifted it over his head. "There you go."

Reaching out tentatively, she let her palm rest in the middle of his chest. Just that soft touch made him feel as if he was going to explode . . . but he kept perfectly still.

"What do you want me to do?" she asked softly.

"Anything you want."

At that, she smiled and slid her fingers into his chest hair, finding his nipple under the mat, running her thumb around it.

"You're awfully good at this," he growled, sucking in a breath.

"You like it?"

"Oh, I like it."

Then his hand was moving up her body and he was cupping her breasts. She was wearing a bra that seemed almost nonexistent. The material was like gossamer. As he cupped her breast in his palm, he heard her soft sigh. Her nipple was already taut, waiting for his touch. When he rubbed the heel of his hand around . . . against it, she moaned.

Laying her back on the sofa, he stretched out on top of her. "You make me crazy," he admitted, kissing her mouth, then her chin, then her neck, until the neckline of her sweater stopped him. She had her arms wrapped around him and was stroking his back. When her fingertips dipped beneath the waistband of his jeans, he shuddered.

Rising on his forearms, he peered down at her. "We've got to stop," he said hoarsely.

"Why?"

"Because I'm getting pretty riled, and I don't think you're ready for this. I don't know if *I'm* ready for this. Fantasizing about it is one thing. Doing it is another. If we finish what we've started here, everything will change between us. I'm not sure we've known each other long enough for that."

"You're afraid if everything changes, you'll want me to leave."

"I'm afraid if everything changes, you'll

want to leave. You're twenty-two. You're a virgin. You have your future ahead of you."

"And you're thirty-four, with your future ahead of *you.* I don't see the conflict."

Verity knew how to turn his reason around on him and he had to admire that. Placing a gentle kiss on her forehead, he levered himself up and moved to the edge of the sofa.

She did the same, and then with a cautious glance she asked, "Where do we go from here?"

"We take one day at a time. We spend more time together. What are you doing for Christmas?" It was two weeks away, and Verity hadn't talked about any plans.

"I don't know."

"Well, I do. I want you to spend it with me and Heather. We're having dinner at Jolene's on Christmas Eve, and I want you to come along as my date."

She grinned at him. "You're going to make an announcement?"

"If need be. But in the meantime, I'm going to pilot Parelli's boat over to Port Aransas next week. Why don't you come along with me? We can stay overnight and fly back in the morning. I told Jolene I'll take the boys for a weekend in January so she and Tim can get away. So I don't think she'll mind taking Heather overnight."

"Heather would stay there?"

"She has before. Or sometimes Jolene brings the kids and stays here. It's like going camping for them. What do you think?"

She didn't hesitate. "I think I'd love to go with you."

He knew he was playing with fire taking her to Port Aransas and spending the night there. But he'd reserve separate rooms. He knew his boundaries, and he'd keep them . . . until he was sure they both knew exactly what they wanted.

As Leo drove Verity to the college Thursday evening to drop off her course selections for next semester, she sneaked a quick glance at him. After they'd watched Heather's program together this morning, he'd asked her if she wanted to go out for dinner to Heather's favorite restaurant where his daughter could eat her favorite meal — chicken and ice cream. When Verity told him she intended to run an errand at the college, he'd insisted he could drive her there on the way to dinner. Looking forward to tonight, she'd relived their evening in the pool house every spare moment. Although she understood he had called a halt to their lovemaking that night because he didn't want to rush her, she also knew he'd stopped because he wasn't sure they belonged together.

The difference in their ages didn't mean a thing to her, but she *was* concerned about his connection to Carolyn. She was even more concerned that the physical attraction he felt was all there was. He was obviously a virile man with strong needs, and she was there . . . handy . . . convenient. If he wasn't invested in more than a physical attraction, he'd walk away like Matthew had.

Since Monday night she'd felt close to Leo, as if they were on the verge of something important. They'd shared a few good night kisses since then, but Leo had kept those kisses under strict control. Oh, how she wished she had someone to confide in. At times like these, she missed Sean the most.

In her car seat, Heather was babbling to Nosy who was propped beside her.

"She took a nap in her new bed without a fuss today," Verity told Leo, choosing a safe topic. "I think she likes it."

"She likes it because you made it special." His gaze as he glanced at her was filled with warmth, and Verity found herself looking forward to the future in a way she hadn't before.

In front of the Arts and Sciences Building there was a curb with spaces slotted for parking. Students were gone for the holidays so parking wasn't a problem.

"Are you sure your advisor will be here?" Leo asked her.

"If he's not, I can just slide the papers under his door." She unfastened her seat belt. "I'll try not to be too long. I don't want Heather to get restless."

"If she gets antsy, I'll take her for a walk. Don't worry about us."

One of the qualities Verity admired most about Leo was his patience. He made her feel as if she was worth waiting for. With a smile she left his SUV and shut the door.

Verity opened the heavy glass door and took the steps leading to the second floor of the Arts and Sciences Building. The halls were quiet and the tile smelled of fresh wax. She couldn't wait until next semester when she'd be involved in her new classes. She'd talked to Leo about it, wondering if being gone two nights a week would be a problem. But he'd been fine with what she'd planned. He'd told her he'd make sure he was home early on those evenings.

She didn't want to be naive about what was happening between them. She didn't want to wear rose-colored glasses only to have them smashed.

When she reached Will Stratford's door, she saw he was in the process of slipping into a jacket. She rapped softly and he opened the door.

"You caught me just in time," he said. He nodded to the envelope in her hand. "Is that everything I need for next semester?"

"I hope so. I scheduled two courses. I hope I'm not biting off more than I can chew."

"Are you worried about the time it'll take to do the work for them?"

"That's part of it. I really want to do this. I've always intended to get my master's. But Leo and I are becoming more involved and —" She stopped abruptly, not knowing whether she should go on or not.

"You want to have time for him, too." Obviously, Will understood. "Yes."

"That's understandable. But you know, no matter what happens between the two of you, you have to make yourself happy. You have to be true to yourself before you can be true to anyone else."

"To thine own self be true," she murmured.

" 'And it must follow, as the night the day, Thou canst not then be false to any man,' " Will finished.

"There's wisdom in Shakespeare's work. *Hamlet*, wasn't it?"

"Someone taught you well," he remarked with that kind smile of his.

"I loved his sonnets best," she confided.

"Don't use the past tense. You can read them anytime you want." He looked thoughtfully at his shelf with its volumes of Shakespearean works. "Are you familiar with *Twelfth Night*?"

"Not really."

"You might want to read it. The heroine, Viola, has a twin, Sebastian. She loses him for a while, then finds him again."

"What does the title mean?"

"The Twelfth Night is the last day of the Christmas season. Historians believe Shakespeare wrote the play for a Twelfth Night celebration. Like most of his comedies, it's about couples in love. You'd probably enjoy it."

Crossing to the door, he said, "Come on. I'll walk you downstairs. I have to stop in the language lab on the first floor. I'm picking up a set of Italian tapes."

"You're going to learn how to speak Italian?"

"I'm hoping to learn enough to get me by for a trip. I'm planning it for spring break."

They went down the staircase together. "How wonderful. I've heard there are so many treasures there to see — the architecture, the artwork, the history."

"You want to tour the world someday?" he asked, amused.

"I don't know. Sometimes I think people look all over the world when what they need is in their own backyard. I'm taking a trip with Leo to Port Aransas next week. I've never been there before."

After the last step, Will turned to her. "You're serious about this man, aren't you?"

"Oh, yes. I just don't know how serious he is about me, if he feels any of what I'm feeling."

Will laid a comforting hand on her shoulder. "Men aren't as quick to accept the whisperings of their heart as women are."

"Do you think men and women are really that different?"

"Oh, I think they're different, until somehow they find the same wave length."

He dropped his hand from her shoulder. "Only nine days till Christmas. If I don't see you before, you have a good holiday."

"Thank you. I will. Will you be going out of town?"

"No. Believe it or not, I'll be cooking Christmas dinner. I have a few friends who are usually at loose ends on holidays, so we spend them together."

Verity thought of the envelope she'd received from her father yesterday with her mail in it. She'd dumped the pieces out looking for a note from her dad. She hadn't found one. Nothing else had looked important to her, not even the envelope from the production company. She certainly wasn't interested in making another commercial. She'd put everything aside because she was hurt her dad hadn't written a note. Maybe deep down, she'd hoped he'd change his mind about spending Christmas with a friend rather than her. She *wanted* to spend Christmas with Leo and Heather, but her heart ached because she wouldn't be seeing her dad this holiday when they'd both be missing Sean. Maybe that's why her father wanted to do something different . . . to run away from the pain. Maybe he wanted to run away from her.

After wishing Will a merry Christmas,

Verity opened the door and went outside.

Leo had unfastened Heather from her car seat and carried her to the sidewalk. As dusk fell, he took her hand, and they walked around a row of loblolly pines to look at the Christmas decorations on the side of the Arts and Sciences Building. There was a replica of a long-horned steer pulling Santa's sleigh. The little old man was wearing a cowboy hat.

Suddenly the display was alight with red and green and white bulbs.

Heather pointed to it and giggled, and he scooped her up into his arms. "Santa's going to come and visit you."

"Vewitee said I haf to be good."

He chuckled. "You're always good."

"Not when I haf to sit in time-out."

"Does that happen with Verity or at pre-school?"

"Bof."

His daughter hadn't even hesitated to tell him the truth, and that pleased him. "Do you want to walk by yourself or do you want me to carry you?"

"You cawwy me."

Leo's cell phone rang a short way from his car. Hefting Heather into one arm, he pulled his phone from his pocket and

163

greeted the caller.

"It's me," Jolene said, "returning your call. What's up, brother dear?"

"I have to take a boat to Port Aransas next week, and I've asked Verity to go with me. How does your schedule look? Can you watch Heather?"

There was silence at the other end. "You asked Verity to go along?"

"Yes," he answered, wanting to face this subject head-on if it was going to be a problem.

"I think that's a great idea. Are you staying overnight?"

Leo felt a bit stunned at Jolene's attitude. "Yes, we are."

"Great. I'll just bring the boys to your place and we'll camp out. I want to see Heather's new bed. Joey and Randy love your big-screen TV. They'll bring their DVDs and have a blast. Knowing Tim, he'll take a dip in the pool."

"This time of year?"

"You know Tim. He loves to swim."

"I hope you don't mind, but I also asked Verity to spend Christmas with us."

"Why would I mind? I like Verity. I hired her."

"That's the point. You *hired* her. But she's become more than a nanny."

"You know what I say to that? Bravo! Do you know how long I've been waiting for you to wake up and take notice of a woman again?"

When he didn't respond, she went on. "You've got a lot of wonderful years ahead of you, Leo."

"I know that. But I don't want to make a mistake. Verity's young."

"Verity's *younger.* She's not young. Don't use that as an excuse to act like a monk."

"Jolene . . ."

"All right. Talking sex with your sister is a little bit sticky. But I've seen you and Verity together. There's enough wattage there to light up all the Christmas trees in Avon Lake."

Leo had turned toward the building, and now he saw Verity coming down the stairs inside the door. There was someone with her — a man, though he couldn't see details because of the shadows — and they seemed quite involved in a conversation.

"I've got to go, Jolene. I'll give you a call when I decide all the details on the trip."

"You do that. I'll talk to you soon."

After Leo closed his phone, he stuffed it back in his pocket, all the while watching Verity. He saw the man beside her lay a hand on her shoulder, and she didn't move away.

What the hell was that all about?

He continued watching, noting how close they were standing. Then Verity moved toward the door.

After Leo opened the back door of the car and settled Heather in her car seat once more, he went around to the driver's side and climbed in.

A few moments later, Verity was sliding in, too.

"Everything all taken care of?" he asked her.

"Yep."

"Did you run into someone when you were coming out?"

"It was my advisor."

She looked a bit embarrassed when she said it, and her cheeks were rosy. If she'd been talking to her advisor, why would she be self-conscious about that? But he didn't ask any more questions. He simply wondered if she was telling him the truth.

"Did you see Leo's face when I came to the door with the kids and said *he* was going to be babysitting and *we* were going shopping?" Jolene asked Verity on

166

Saturday as they strolled into a fashion store at the mall.

Verity laughed. "I don't think he really minded."

"No, I don't, either. He loves kids. He should have a whole mess of them."

Verity kept silent as Jolene found a rack of matching slacks and tops, then poked through it. She selected a red set in Verity's size and winked. "This should get him revved up."

"Jolene," Verity protested.

"Oh, honey. Aren't you absolutely excited about this trip?"

"I guess it shows."

"Sure, it does, and I'm glad. Leo actually looked happy today. I can't tell you the last time he really looked forward to something." Holding the outfit in front of Verity, she closed one eye and appeared to be imagining Verity in it. "Yep. This will work. Did you ever think of wearing contact lenses?"

"I tried them for a while."

"What happened?"

"They were soft contacts and one of them tore. I never had them replaced because I hadn't bought the insurance. I was saving money for a car and they just seemed frivolous."

"You should think about wearing them again . . . maybe having your hair styled."

As Jolene studied her even more closely, Verity asked, "What?"

"I can't put my finger on it, but something about you seems familiar."

"Maybe you're just seeing too much of me."

Jolene shook her head, obviously trying to remember. "Maybe you just look like someone else I know. Leo told me you're going to be sharing Christmas Eve with us."

"I hope that's okay."

"It's fine with me. But Mom's going to be there, too, so prepare yourself."

"I'm not exactly sure how to prepare myself for your mother."

At that, Jolene shook her head and laughed. "Isn't that the truth! At least this time *I'm* making dinner and you don't have to worry about preparing anything."

"But I want to. I want to help, anyway. I can make pies — chocolate cream, maybe?"

Jolene groaned. "You've found my weakness. All right. You go to it. And if you come over early, you can keep me from going crazy when my mom tries to tell me how to cook a meal I've made at least once a year for the past eleven years."

"Three women in the kitchen could be a nightmare," Verity warned.

"Yep. Close to it," Jolene agreed. "That's why I'll convince Leo and Tim to tell her all about their work and anything else they can think of until we get dinner on the table." Jolene wiggled the red sweater in front of Verity's nose. "But for right now, let's get you dressed to have a little fun."

There was no harm in buying a sweater and a pair of slacks, Verity told herself. She hadn't bought new clothes in months. If Leo liked her in the outfit, maybe she would find her tomboy days were definitely over. As the thought came and went, she almost believed she could hear her twin's voice whispering *"Atta girl."*

With alacrity, she took the slacks and sweater from Jolene and headed for the dressing room.

Chapter Eight

Aboard Mr. Parelli's cabin cruiser the following Tuesday, Verity looked around in admiration. The boat was fantastic. Leo had given her the statistics before they'd climbed onboard. It was a twenty-seven-footer with a large V-berth bed. All of its other fittings — the wraparound side seats, the built-in ice chest, the sink, icebox and head — had floated around her as Leo had described it so proudly. Although the boat was beautiful, she hadn't been able to take her eyes off *him* in his green T-shirt and gray stone-washed jeans. When he'd given her a tour and shown her the bed, her imagination had worked overtime.

Now sitting on one of the side seats, Verity watched Leo at the wheel. He'd explained the boat could practically navigate itself on autopilot. Still, he looked as if he belonged there — stoic, stalwart and strong.

The wind tugged strands of hair free from Verity's ponytail as she looked out to sea and wondered if she'd been approaching Leo all wrong. This time they were spending alone together could be important. Maybe she should confront the issues between them head-on instead of dancing around them. What did she have to lose?

They'd been on the water for most of the morning when she asked him, "How about some lunch? I can bring it up here."

Without looking at her, with his gaze still on the sea, he said, "Sounds good."

Ten minutes later Verity carried tall cups of iced tea to the control deck and set them in the holders by the seats. When she returned again, she juggled two paper plates that held thick roast beef sandwiches, macaroni salad, chips and carrot strips.

Leo swiveled around on one of the bucket seats while she sat on the side bench.

When his gaze met hers, it was like two firecrackers colliding and exploding. She practically shook from the power of their attraction, but forced herself to remain calm, to smile, as his hungry gaze passed over her red slacks and sweater.

"Do you get to do this often?" she asked, as if her insides weren't quaking.

"Pilot a customer's boat?" he asked.

"Yes. Deliver it this way."

"Maybe a quarter of the time. Usually the proud owner can't wait to get his hands on the boat, and he wants to navigate it himself."

"Do you own a boat?" she asked. It seemed only logical, after all, since he built them.

"Yes, I do. One much like this one. But it's in dry dock right now."

"Being repaired?"

"No. I realized I hadn't taken it out for about a year. I decided to have the controls updated."

She guessed dry dock had nothing to do with new controls. Not really. After his wife died, he'd withdrawn from life, too, just as she had.

"I guess you haven't had much time to go boating. Not with full responsibility for Heather and all. Did your wife enjoy boats as much as you do?"

With his sandwich halfway to his mouth, Leo stopped and laid it back on his plate. His sharp look almost made Verity lose her courage; nevertheless, she kept her gaze on his.

After a few very long moments, he admitted, "Carolyn didn't like to set foot on boats. She always got seasick."

"So you didn't take excursions together

before Heather was born?" Verity thought about that V-berth bed, and how exciting and cozy making love on the water would be.

"No excursions. When we were engaged, I brought Carolyn out, just for a short jaunt. She got terribly seasick. After that, we tried it once more. Even though she took medication before we left, that didn't help, either. She decided boats just weren't in her karma."

"That must have been lonely for you, with you loving the water so much — being torn between wanting to go out on the sea or spend time with her."

A shadow passed over his face. "Verity, this isn't something I want to talk about."

"Why? Because it hurts?" She was pushing, and she knew it.

With a thump, Leo set his plate on the deck. "I don't want to talk about it because it's in the past."

"You can't forget the past, Leo. It's a shadow, always dogging you."

After a short silence he answered, "I suppose you're right. But just because I have a shadow, doesn't mean I want to dissect it."

"The past or your marriage?"

Now Leo stood and braced himself

against the rocking of the boat. "My marriage isn't something I want to discuss with *you.*"

His statement hurt, but she wasn't sorry she'd asked the questions. The subject of Carolyn was obviously a minefield. As long as it was, they wouldn't be able to move on, or move deeper into any kind of relationship.

"You say you don't want to talk about it with me, Leo. Why is that? Do you talk about it with anyone? Jolene?"

"My marriage is over. I can't fix what it was or wasn't by discussing it."

"Why would you want to fix it?" she asked quietly.

"Enough, Verity," he said curtly, turning away from her and checking the instruments.

He obviously thought he was shutting her down . . . shutting off the conversation. As she took a sip of her iced tea and watched his chiseled profile against the blue sky, she wondered if she'd done damage or good. Maybe she'd find out after they arrived in Port Aransas.

A few hours later, Verity watched Leo as they came into port, fascinated by the masterful way he handled the boat, how he easily and expertly backed it into a slip at the marina. A man on the dock helped him tie it down, and Verity suddenly wished she knew how to do all of the things that Leo needed help with. She'd like to be able to crew for him. Apparently he was used to doing this alone. He was used to doing a lot of things alone.

There was a car waiting for them in the marina's parking lot. Mr. Parelli had arranged for it to be there.

After putting their bags in the trunk, Leo held the door of the blue sedan as Verity climbed in. At her murmured thanks, he gave her a small smile, but it didn't reach his eyes. Their conversation about his wife had made the walls between them even higher and thicker. That wasn't at all what she'd planned.

The resort where they'd be staying wasn't far. When they turned into the drive, Verity saw the sprawling hotel, the rambling golf course, the lush vegetation encouraged even in December. Mexican fans and queen palms dotted the front lawn.

Leo parked and escorted her inside to a lobby. Soft music played, and their footsteps were muffled by velvety teal carpet. The reception counter was beautifully polished wood. Groupings of furniture in splashes of blue, peach and green looked comfortable and elegant. Checking in took only a few minutes, then Leo carried his duffel bag and her valise to the elevator.

When they rose to the third floor in silence, Verity wished she knew what he was thinking. She wished she knew why he'd asked her along.

In the intimacy of the elevator, silence grew long and tense until Leo asked, "Would you feel comfortable going riding on the beach?"

She remembered the painting in her sitting room and her dreams concerning it. "I'd love to go riding on the beach, as long as you don't challenge me to a race. I'm not sure I could stay in the saddle."

"No racing," he assured her, "just a leisurely walk, if that's all you want. Riding on the beach is much different from taking a trail ride. Especially at night. I checked and there's a full moon. If the fog rolls in, we might have to think about something else."

If the fog rolled in, she could think of a thousand things she and Leo could do, all of them making her blush.

Verity had watched the clerk at the desk give Leo two folders with keys. Now, as they came to one of the doors, he set down her valise and his duffel bag, reaching into his pocket for one of the small folders. "I'll go inside with you to see if everything's okay."

After he used the keycard, he let her precede him into the room. When he followed her, he laid her suitcase on the low chest next to the mirrored dresser.

The room had a nautical theme with a seascape mural wallpapered to one wall. The spreads were patterned with palm trees and surfboards, and drapes at the window were a pretty palm green over cream sheers.

Crossing to the window, Leo opened the blind to let sunlight pour in. Cerulean sky met green-blue water, and the view was absolutely breathtaking.

"Do you come here often?" she asked Leo, wondering if he'd ever brought his wife here.

"I stayed here once before when I came on business. There's a fine restaurant downstairs."

As she turned from the window, her gaze fell on the king-size bed. When she looked up, she found Leo studying her.

He motioned to a door across from the bathroom. "That connects your room and mine. But you can keep it locked if that makes you feel more comfortable."

"Did you request connecting rooms?" she asked, the idea giving her a thrill. Maybe Leo wanted tonight to be more than a minivacation.

"No, I didn't. But I did request sea-view rooms."

"Oh," she murmured.

Her soft exclamation must have held a note of disappointment, because Leo set his duffel on the bed and came to stand before her. Catching a strand of hair that had come loose from her ponytail, his fingers slid down it sensually, and he touched it as if he was enjoying the silky feel of it. "I asked you along on this trip so we could get to know each other better, not so I could take advantage of you. I don't want you to feel uncomfortable in any way."

"I only feel uncomfortable when you close down on me," she admitted.

He stopped fingering her hair and looked puzzled. "Close down on you?"

"You withdraw, Leo, when we broach a subject you don't want to talk about. If we get in the middle of something sticky, you turn off. You go somewhere where I can't reach you."

His silence was loud in the room until he

asked, "You mean our conversation on the boat?"

"You shut down when we talk about Carolyn."

For a moment she thought he was going to do exactly what he had done on the boat and other times — close the door on the subject.

This time he didn't. "I wasn't aware I was doing that. I wasn't aware I was shutting you out." Encircling her with his arms, he tugged her close. "I guess I've gotten used to being alone. I've gotten used to keeping my distance from Jolene when she wants to give me advice, and walling Mother off when she tries to manipulate me into doing something she wants."

Feeling closer to Leo now, Verity asked, "Did you do it with Carolyn, too?"

When he tensed, she reached up and stroked his jaw.

Relaxing again, he turned his head and kissed her palm. The feel of his lips on her skin sent a thrill through her.

"Maybe I did," he admitted hoarsely. After a pause he added, "When I'm with you, Verity, I don't want walls between us." Tipping her chin up, he gave her a long, slow kiss.

After he released her, he asked, "Do you

want to explore the grounds before dinner?"

His kisses always made her dizzy, made her dreams swirl around her like a cloud she couldn't grasp. She nodded.

"I have to put in a call to Parelli. Then we can go out."

Leo went to the connecting door, unlocked and opened it, then disappeared.

Verity thought about those connecting doors and what they could mean. One thing she knew — she wouldn't be locking hers.

Leo on horseback was even sexier than Leo on his boat, Verity thought, as they rode across the sand. The night was perfect, the sky an immense black canopy lit up by an almost-full moon and thousands of stars. They'd eaten a candlelit dinner at the restaurant, talked about Heather, places they'd traveled, funny stories from their childhoods. Memories of Sean had surfaced, and as Verity had shared them with Leo, she felt even closer to him. She'd told him about shooting stars and how she believed seeing one would be a message from Sean. Leo had told her about the night Heather was born, how watching her come into the world had been incomparable to anything else in his life.

As she'd sipped coffee, his gaze had lingered on her face. When they'd shared a fudgy, brownie dessert, their forks had touched, they'd both gone silent and she'd glimpsed the hungry desire in Leo's eyes.

Now, on the beach, she rode beside him, managing to keep up. As waves crashed on the shore, Leo led her just above them and came to a stop.

When she pulled up beside him, he asked, "Do you want to walk the beach?"

She remembered the night of his company party and thought about how much closer they were now. "Yes," she answered, hoping tonight would be the absolutely best night of her life.

Leo dismounted quickly, then held her horse while she slipped off. They hadn't gone very far when she saw lights appear on the horizon.

Stopping, they gazed out to sea together. "That looks big," she said, "but not as large as a cruise ship."

"It's probably a private yacht."

"Did you ever want a yacht of your own? You could build yourself one."

He laughed. "Yes, I could, I guess. But I never wanted a yacht. I did want to sail around the world, though, and I still might, after Heather's grown."

"Do you want to sail alone?"

Instead of looking out into the black night and the sea, he was suddenly looking at her. "I thought I did. I thought the solitude would be wonderful. But now I'm wondering if solitude is really what I want."

"Do you think you'd like to take someone along?"

"I'd like to take someone along who could enjoy the adventure as much as I would."

"I loved coming over here on your boat, if that means anything."

Closer now, he looked as if he might kiss her. But then his horse pulled on the reins, and he just draped an arm around her shoulders instead. "I think you'd be good company."

She wanted to be so much more than company, but Leo was still holding back, and maybe she was, too. Were their pasts tying them up again?

"You have a dream to sail around the world," she said softly. "Do you have other dreams?"

"I want to expand the boatyard. I want to fulfill dreams my father couldn't and make him proud."

"I'm sure your father is already very proud. Do you believe he's watching over you?"

"I believe he is, just as your twin's watching over you."

Their hips bumped as they walked, and Verity loved the contact with Leo, the intimacy of touching, walking side by side and being comfortable with him. She'd worn a jacket and was glad of that now as the sea mist sprayed across the beach. Leo's arm around her kept her warm, and whenever their gazes met, her temperature went up another five degrees.

"Tell me about your dad," Leo suggested. "You don't talk about him much, and I have to wonder why you're not spending Christmas with him."

"He's spending Christmas with a friend." Then she added, "He seemed relieved I wasn't coming home."

"Why would he be relieved? If he raised you and your brother on his own, I'd imagine the three of you would be tight."

Memories flooded back. As the sea air brushed her face, she explained, "Sean and Dad always had a connection. It was as if I came along with the package. I guess that's why I was a tomboy as a kid. If I tagged along with Sean and played sports with him, my father seemed to know I was around."

After a pause Leo admitted, "At times I do think it would be easier to raise a boy. When I think ahead, I can't imagine talking to Heather about everything a mother would tell a daughter."

"You mean bras and boys?" Verity teased.

Leo grinned down at her wryly. "Exactly. So, I can understand how your dad probably felt. Yet I also know, as a single parent, I have the responsibility to talk to her about everything, whether I'm comfortable with it or not."

"Sean had always been the buffer between Dad and me. He smoothed conversations between us. After he was gone, it was as if Dad had nothing to say to me. Neither of us seemed to be able to talk about how much we missed Sean, and this silence grew between us until it was so big it pushed us farther and farther away from each other. I know how much he loved Sean, and when we're together, I feel I'm a reminder that my brother's not here."

As Leo's arm around her tightened, he stopped walking and pulled her to him for a hug. When he leaned away, he suggested, "Why don't you ask your dad to come to

Avon Lake for Christmas?"

"He already has plans."

"Maybe he made those plans because it was the easier thing to do. But if you gave him an alternative, I can't imagine he'd want to be with a friend on Christmas rather than with his daughter."

If she gave her father the alternative and he didn't take it, then she'd know for sure he didn't want to be with her.

"I don't think you should let the holiday go by without making contact," Leo went on. "If you do, the chasm between you will become even wider. Don't you think?"

She knew Leo was probably right, yet she didn't know if she had the courage to face rejection again.

"Think about it," he suggested.

In the moonlight Leo's strong features seemed even more handsome. He wasn't wearing a jacket, and his polo shirt was open at the neck. The chest hair there tempted her to touch it. She wanted to touch *him*. Everywhere. The way he was looking at her, she guessed he wanted the same thing.

However, instead of kissing her, he said, "We'd better head back. It's getting late." After he released her, he took her horse's reins from her hands. "Come on.

I'll give you a lift up."

After Leo helped her mount, they started back to the resort. Suddenly Verity saw it — a bright streak against the black sky — a shooting star.

Smiling, she now knew Sean was watching over her. He was sending her a message — he approved of her relationship with Leo.

She was ready for the next step.

An hour later Verity closed the volume of *Twelfth Night* she'd borrowed from the library, too distracted to read. She knew why. She'd missed her chance. She hadn't been bold enough.

After their ride Leo had walked her to her room, kissed her on the forehead and said he'd see her in the morning. She'd simply accepted all of that, when what she'd wanted was to be held in his arms. He thought he had to go slowly because she was a virgin. He thought he had to go slowly because she was younger than he was. He thought he had to go slowly be-cause . . . because he might not be ready for a new involvement.

She already knew Leo was a man of in-tegrity who wanted to be sure of every step he took. If he only knew how much she cared about him.

There was only one way he was going to know — she had to show him.

She'd brought along a pale-pink silk chemise for sleeping. She usually wore pajamas, but this had been a present from her aunt last Christmas, and bringing it along had seemed appropriate. It had come with a flowered, pink-and-green silk robe, and now she slipped from the bed and put on the robe, belting it at her waist. She thought about leaving her glasses in the room, but she wanted to see Leo's expression. He had a way of drawing his thick brows together as he pondered something. When he really smiled, the lines around his mouth deepened. Most of all, she wanted to watch his eyes, which were often as mysterious as the sea.

She knew if she thought too long about what she intended to do, she'd lose her courage, so instead of considering her actions another moment, she opened the connecting door and stepped into Leo's room.

A dim light glowed beside Leo's bed. He was stretched out on top of the covers, shirtless, wearing black shorts. There was so much tanned skin! His muscles looked powerful, and she was in awe of his male body which seemed perfect to her.

"Verity?" he asked, a multitude of questions in the sound of her name.

Frozen for an instant, she finally pulled herself together and stepped deeper into the room and closer to him. "Our good night was so short, I thought maybe you'd like to do it over again." The last two words had wobbled a bit, but she'd gotten them out.

Leo's gaze absorbed everything about her, then lingered on the robe and the way the fabric molded to her. "This isn't a good idea." His voice was rough.

Taking a few more steps closer to the bed, she asked almost in a whisper, "Do you want me?"

His groan was deep and heartfelt and brought a half smile to his lips. "Oh, Verity, if only you knew."

"If only I knew what?"

"If only you knew how hard it was for me to keep my hands off you on the beach. If only you knew how hard it was just to give you a kiss on the forehead good night. Now here you are, all soft and willing, and I'm trying to be a gentleman about the whole thing."

"Don't gentlemen make love?"

He laughed. "I suppose so. But they don't talk about it much."

"No kissing and telling?" she teased, her heart racing.

Taking her hand, Leo sat on the edge of the bed and drew her down beside him. "When a man's serious about a woman, he keeps his thoughts private."

"Are you serious about me?" She had to know if she was making a fool of herself.

"I'm attracted to you, Verity. But I don't know if I'm ready for serious. I can't make love to you until I'm prepared to make a commitment, and *I'm* not ready for that yet, either. I don't want you to tie yourself down to me and my baggage. It's as simple as that."

"But you brought me along so we could get to know each other better. And we have. Tonight on the beach, we were close."

"Yes, we were. I feel a bond with you I don't understand."

"Then stop fighting it."

"Is that what I'm doing?" His voice held a touch of humor.

"Yes, I think you are. I think you feel guilty because you're beginning to have feelings for me, yet part of you still feels married. I think you've found something with me you didn't find with your wife, and you're wondering why that's so. You're thinking too much, Leo, instead of feeling."

Now he turned completely serious. "It's not that easy."

"It could be. It could be as easy as making the decision to go on with your life."

"When you're older and more experienced, Verity —"

Tears sprang to her eyes. "You're trying to find every excuse in the book."

Standing, she blinked, refusing to cry in front of him. "I shouldn't have come in here, Leo. Maybe that *is* inexperience. I thought we could come together as equals, but you don't see me as an equal. Until you do, we *don't* belong together."

She'd left the door between their rooms open when she'd walked in. Now, as she exited Leo's room, she closed it behind her. She didn't try to hold back tears. She was ready to take a voyage with Leo, no matter where it would lead. But at this point his baggage would sink them.

Taking off her robe and glasses, she laid them aside, then slipped between the sheets. After she turned off the light, she curled on her side and thought about all the preparations she'd make for Christmas. She had almost finished her present for

Leo — a memory book that included photos of Heather over the past year. She'd taken pictures she'd found in the closet to an office supply store and had duplicates made. She'd finish the present in the next day or two.

Only four days till Christmas.

Her Christmas wish for Leo was an unfettered heart. Until he was free of his past, he wouldn't be able to return her love.

How long would she have to wait?

Chapter Nine

"Jingle bells, jingle bells, jingle all the way." Heather sang along with Verity as Verity slipped a stretchy bracelet surrounded by bells onto Heather's wrist. With a giggle Heather shook her hand and made them ring. She was dressed in a red velvet jumper with a satiny, puffy-sleeved white blouse, and looked absolutely adorable.

"You jingle, too," Heather directed, pointing to Verity's bracelet, which was just like hers.

With a grin, Verity shook her wrist. She'd bought the bracelets, knowing Heather would like the sound of the bells.

Leo poked his head into Heather's room. "Ready?" When his gaze landed on his daughter, he smiled. Then his attention shifted to Verity.

She'd dressed in green wool slacks and a cream, silky blouse, and now as Leo appraised her, the heat in his gaze warmed her all over. The past few days had been difficult because of the way she'd left Leo's room at Port Aransas. They hadn't said anything further on the subject, and it was like the proverbial elephant in the room. They walked around it, talked around it and pretended to ignore it. But there it was.

On their return from their overnight stay, she'd concentrated on making the holidays special for Heather — and Leo — from the wire wreath on the door, with its pine cones at the top of the circle and a cutout of the state of Texas at the bottom, to the red candles on the mantel and the pies she'd baked to take along to Jolene's tonight.

"I've loaded everything into the car," Leo said now.

When the doorbell rang, Verity glanced at him. "Are you expecting someone?"

"No. How about you?"

She shook her head.

"I'll get it," Leo offered. "You can make sure we didn't forget anything."

A few minutes later Verity was helping Heather slip on a jacket when Leo returned to the room with a man following him. Her father!

"Dad! What are you doing here?"

Her father looked ill at ease and uncertain. "You called and left that message."

That message.

After her talk with Leo on the beach at Port Aransas, she had decided to take one more step at communicating with her father. But when she'd called, he hadn't been home. She'd left a simple message: "Dad — If your plans fall through or you change your mind about how you'd like to spend Christmas, I'd be happy to spend it with you. You can come here or I can come home. Just let me know."

He hadn't returned her call. "When you didn't call back, I figured your original plans stood."

"I got to thinking. We haven't spent much time together lately."

"We never did spend much time together." A mixture of emotions washed over her as she said it. She wanted to spend Christmas Eve with Leo and Heather and Jolene and her family, yet her father was the only family she had left, and she wanted desperately to forge bonds with him, too. She just didn't know how. "Did you check in at a motel?"

"Not yet. I passed a nice one. But I wanted to see if you were even here."

"There's no need for you to stay at a motel," Leo interjected, scooping Heather up into his arms. "I have a spare room, and you're welcome to it."

"I don't want to impose," her father stated firmly.

"You're not imposing. In fact, you can come along to my sister's for Christmas Eve dinner."

"Leo, I don't know about that . . ." Verity began, thinking about Leo's mother who would also be there and her possible comments about a stranger joining in.

Heather reached her arms out to Verity. "Cawwy me?"

Verity looked from Heather and Leo to her father. What would her dad think about all of it? Would he be uncomfortable with Jolene and her family?

She wasn't sure what the best thing was to do, so she decided to leave it in her dad's hands. "Dad, it's up to you. The two of us can go out, or you can come along."

Looking uncertain, Gregory Sumpter finally turned to Leo. "You're sure your sister won't mind?"

"I'm absolutely sure."

"Do *you* mind if I come along?" he asked Verity.

"No, I don't mind. The celebration might get a little rowdy."

"Rowdy's fine on Christmas Eve," he said with a smile. "In fact, I remember that Christmas Eve that Sean —" He stopped abruptly, and the old awkwardness and tension returned between them.

She finished for him. "The Christmas Eve Sean brought the whole basketball team home for supper. Yep, that was rowdy," she agreed lightly, then gathered Heather into her arms and hugged her close. The sweet-little-girl smell of her comforted Verity somehow. Maybe with enough people around, the awkwardness between her and her dad would dissipate some. She hoped so, or it was going to be a very long Christmas Eve.

At Jolene's house, Christmas Eve dinner became organized chaos, but Verity loved it. She couldn't remember ever being part of a holiday like this. Her father seemed a bit befuddled by all of it — the kids running around, the adults having conversations over their heads, the wonderful smells drifting into the living room from the kitchen. Verity soaked it all in, glanced at her father and Leo often, and felt as if her life were changing on all fronts.

Leo's mother was late, and Leo explained that that was a common occurrence, even on Christmas Eve.

Finally the doorbell to Jolene's ranch house rang. Tim hurried to answer it, and when he returned to the living room, Amelia Montgomery accompanied him . . .

and so did another, younger woman.

"Hi, everyone." Amelia greeted them all with a wide smile. "Leo, look who I bumped into this week. She said she didn't have anyplace to go tonight, so I invited her along. I thought you two could catch up."

Jolene, who was sitting beside Verity on the sofa leaned over and out of the side of her mouth whispered, "Marjorie and Leo went to high school together. She's a stock broker."

The woman Amelia Montgomery had brought along was absolutely exquisite, with short black hair that looked to be styled by an expert, large green eyes and a model's walk. Verity knew that walk because a coach for the commercial she'd made had taught it to her.

"Everyone," Amelia said, "you remember Marjorie Canfield, don't you?"

Marjorie's gaze had targeted Leo as if she didn't care about anyone else in the room, and Verity felt a bit of panic. Had these two been sweethearts? Had they been involved? If so, did Leo still feel anything for her?

The gentleman that he was, Leo stood and approached Marjorie with a smile. "It's good to see you again. I didn't know you were back in Avon Lake."

"I returned more than a month ago. I bought a leather shop over on Bullhorn Road."

"Tired of big-city life?" Leo asked, as if he were genuinely interested.

"No. But with the financial markets being what they are, I decided to plunge into a less stressful business. Selling leather products in Avon Lake should be a breeze."

Amelia laughed, and then turned her attention to Verity. "Verity Sumpter, meet Marjorie. Marjorie, Verity is Leo's nanny." Her gaze settled on Gregory Sumpter. "And, I don't know who this gentleman is. Jolene?"

After further introductions were made, Verity's father glanced at her often, as if he sensed some kind of triangle had suddenly come into existence.

As Leo sat next to Verity at dinner, his knee grazed hers more than once, their elbows brushed and their hands tangled when they reached for the salt shaker. However, Marjorie was seated on Leo's other side, and Verity caught tidbits of the conversation when Heather wasn't demanding her attention. Leo and Marjorie were obviously catching up. Verity didn't like the way the ex-stockbroker looked at him, as if she could eat him up along with the ham!

When Jolene served Verity's chocolate-cream pies and pumpkin-custard pies for dessert, everyone oohed and aahed over them, except for Amelia and Marjorie, who declined because they were watching their figures.

"I wish my crusts were as light as Verity's," Jolene admitted as she took her first enthusiastic bite of chocolate-cream pie.

"If you ever tire of being a nanny, you could open a bakery," Amelia suggested helpfully.

"I think the fun would go out of baking if I did that," Verity returned politely, realizing Leo's mother was trying to keep her in her place.

"How long do you intend to be a nanny? Do you have any future goals?"

In spite of her vow to herself to keep her equilibrium tonight, Verity felt herself bristling at Amelia's patronizing tone. "My goal is to enjoy any work I do. Taking care of Heather is teaching me more than any degree I could earn."

In explanation, Amelia turned to Marjorie. "Verity is taking courses at the college. Isn't that right, dear?"

Verity took a deep breath and answered, "Yes. For a master's degree. I'm not exactly sure what I'll do with it when I finish. I guess it depends on how long Leo needs me."

At her statement, silence settled over the table for a few moments. Finally conversation started up again, and Verity was relieved.

Tim announced, "As soon as we're finished here, we'll sing Christmas carols around the piano. Then I'll read the 'Christmas Story' before the kids fall asleep."

Little Joey piped up, "I'm not gonna sleep tonight. I'm gonna sit by the tree and wait for Santa."

Tim grinned at his son. "Maybe instead of sitting and waiting, you can go to bed and listen for the bells on his sleigh. I'm afraid he might not come in if he knows you're watching."

After thinking about that, Joey looked at Verity. "Can I leave him a piece of your pie? I think he'd like that better than cookies."

Everyone at the table smiled. "Sure you can leave him a piece of pie. And don't forget the milk to go with it."

"I want to give Santa pie, too," Heather

decided, sliding off her chair and coming over to Verity's side. After a yawn, she laid her head on Verity's lap.

"I think this one's going to be asleep before we get home." Leo's gaze locked on Verity's.

As Leo sat at his sister's table, the woman his mother had handpicked for him on his left and Verity Sumpter on his right, he realized his need for Verity went far beyond any physical satisfaction he could find with her. Verity wanted to be his equal, and he suddenly realized that she was. There was a maturity, compassion and understanding about her that he found few women possessed. Where before doubts had plagued him, they were now replaced with a certainty that she belonged in his life . . . in Heather's life. As Verity stroked Heather's hair, Leo felt more right with the world than he'd felt in a very long time.

While everyone else gathered around the piano to sing Christmas carols, Leo cornered his mother in the hall outside the powder room. Leo could see she'd just made sure every hair was in place and her lipstick freshened.

"Why are you scowling, Leo?" she asked with a smile. "It's Christmas Eve."

"Yes, I know it's Christmas Eve. I'd like to know why you asked Marjorie to join us tonight."

His mother's face reflected complete innocence. "It's simple. She was going to spend the holiday alone. Just recently moving back to town, she hasn't reacquainted herself with her friends. She has no family here anymore. I didn't want her to be alone."

"I think your motive went deeper than that. What did you think would happen when Marjorie and I got together again?"

"You two dated in high school. You're both single. I thought you might find common ground once more. It's time you get on with your life."

His voice was calm but firm. "I *am* getting on with my life. You just don't like the direction it's headed. The type of woman you'd choose to be your daughter-in-law is *not* the type of woman I'd choose to be a wife and mother."

Amelia Montgomery looked stunned for a moment. Actually Leo had never seen her speechless before.

Hearing light footsteps, he looked up and saw Verity coming into the hall. She stopped as soon as she spotted them. "Oh, I'm sorry. I didn't mean to interrupt." In

Verity's considerate way, she turned to leave.

But in two strides Leo was beside her, taking her hand and drawing her toward him. "Mom, I know you're worried about me because you think I should start dating again. Well, I have. I'm dating Verity. In fact, we're going to a concert at the college day after tomorrow."

Verity's eyes grew wide at his announcement, and she didn't seem to know what to say.

To her credit, his mother recovered swiftly. "I didn't know you two were serious." Her eyes were questioning. "I thought Verity just worked for you. After all, you're so much older —"

"I might be older, but Verity's mature. She's faced loss just as I have. Now that you know we're dating, maybe the two of you can get to know each other better."

Quick on the uptake, Verity offered, "You can come to dinner anytime. Just give me a call or drop in."

Amelia looked at her as if she were seeing her in a different light. "I'll do that." With a last glance at the two of them, she went down the hall to join the festivities once more.

"What did I miss?" Verity asked, looking a bit bemused.

"Would you like to go to a concert with me day after tomorrow?"

"Sure. I didn't know if you were just telling your mom that or if you really meant it."

"I meant it."

"Are you sure this isn't just an easy out so you don't have to date Marjorie?" she asked, half joking, half serious.

Taking Verity by the shoulders, Leo looked deep into her eyes. "This has nothing to do with Marjorie." Tipping her chin up, he softly kissed her lips, then added, "This has to do with *us*."

He could see there were still doubts in Verity's eyes, and his goal would be to eliminate them. Dropping his arm around her, he guided her back to the living room. This was going to be the best Christmas he'd ever had.

It was almost midnight when Verity and Leo positioned Heather's presents under Leo's tree.

On the sofa her father turned from the TV where a choir sang Handel's *Messiah*. "Don't forget to put out that pie for Santa," he reminded them. "I'm sure

Heather will look for the empty dish in the morning."

Leo laughed. "I'm sure you're right about that."

"I can get it," Verity offered.

"Why don't we all have a midnight piece of pie before turning in? There's something I need to get in the pool house. I'll be right back."

After Leo had gone, Verity and her father were left in the great room. The lights on the tree twinkled on and off as the smell of pine filled the room.

After positioning the last present perfectly, Verity went to the kitchen doorway. "Would you like a piece of pie, Dad?"

"Sure." After he followed her into the kitchen, he pulled out a chair at the table. "You and Leo are involved, aren't you?"

"We're heading that way," she answered, hoping it was true. At first when she'd come upon Leo and his mother, she'd thought he'd told his mother they were dating simply to avoid her matchmaking. Afterward, however, when he'd looked into her eyes, she'd seen that maybe he *was* ready to move on with his life.

"His little girl seems attached to you," her father noticed.

"Heather and I connected right away."

"You haven't been here very long. Are you sure things aren't moving too fast?"

Words sailed out of her mouth before she could catch them. "You've never cared who I've dated before. Why now?"

Her father lowered himself into the chair. "Because this time it looks serious. Because . . ." He hesitated. "Because this time Sean isn't here to protect you."

"You relied on Sean to protect me?" she asked softly.

"I knew you'd listen to him."

"I would have listened to you, too. In fact, it would have meant everything to me to know you cared about me as much as you did about Sean."

Stunned, her father just stared at her. Eventually he responded almost sternly, "I have *always* cared about you, Verity."

"Not the same way you cared about Sean," she returned quietly.

After a few tense moments, her father ran his hand through his hair. "Sean and I were guys. I didn't know what to do with you. Especially when you started growing up."

"You didn't know what to *do* with me?"

"That didn't come out right," he sighed. "Verity, I was a single dad, and I did my best to give you and your brother guidelines. You were twins, and most of the time you didn't seem to need anyone else. When you were kids, you even had your own language. You did everything together. Remember when I tried to convince you to take dancing lessons and you said you'd only do it if Sean did, too? He wanted no part of it so you never got the lessons."

"I remember."

"That's the kind of thing I'm talking about. I didn't know how to go about helping you do girlie things."

"I didn't *want* to do girlie things. I liked sports. I liked climbing trees and hiking."

Her father shook his head. "I was never sure of that. I was never sure you were finding your own way, not just following in your brother's. But I never cared about you any less than Sean, and once you became a teenager . . . I was *really* out of my element. That's why I asked your aunt to have that talk with you."

That talk. The birds and the bees. Her aunt had come to visit one Easter and had sat her down and explained everything. At least everything she could fit into an hour. Verity had never realized her father had put her aunt up to it.

"I think Aunt April was as uncomfortable as you would have been."

"Maybe. But I would have turned red and stammered through it. I would have needed a script."

"Oh, Dad." Seeing fatherhood through her dad's eyes, considering parenting a boy compared to parenting a girl, Verity understood the difficulties . . . understood in a way she never had before.

"Why didn't you return my call before Thanksgiving? Did you want to spend it alone?"

"I was feeling absolutely raw," her dad admitted. "Ever since we lost Sean, all I wanted to do was crawl in a cave and lick my wounds. I know that was selfish. I know you were hurting as much as I was. But I didn't know how to make us both feel better, so it was just easier to retreat."

"I tried that for a while," Verity confessed. "But it didn't work. I missed Sean more. Since I've come here, though, all of it's been better. I don't know how to explain it, but when I'm playing with Heather, hugging her, it's almost as if Sean's looking over my shoulder. I know that sounds silly —"

"No, it doesn't. As connected as you and your brother were, I know he's looking out for you now. When you called and left that invitation for Christmas on my machine, I knew if we didn't make contact again, I'd lose you as surely as I'd lost Sean."

In the silence Verity knew he was right. Going to her father then, she hugged him. "You're not going to lose me. And we can keep memories of Sean alive by remembering him together."

When Verity leaned away from her dad, she saw his eyes were as moist as hers.

The sliding glass doors from the patio opened, and Leo came into the kitchen.

As if embarrassed by his emotion, Verity's father stepped away from her. "I think I'll turn in," he mumbled.

"Heather will probably be up at the crack of dawn," Leo warned. "Don't feel you have to get up that early."

"And miss the look in your daughter's eyes when she opens her presents?" Verity's father exclaimed. "I don't think so. It's been years since I witnessed a child's wonder. I think I'm ready for a good dose of it again." Then he capped Verity's shoulder and squeezed it. "I'll see you in the morning."

She covered his hand with hers. "Good night, Dad."

When her father had left the kitchen, Leo asked, "Did you two talk?"

"Is that why you left us alone?"

"Partly," he admitted with a smile.

"Yes, we talked. I don't know if we've ever talked exactly like that before. I guess I never realized how hard it was for him to raise me and Sean on his own. Seeing you with Heather has brought some of that home."

As Leo approached her now, she saw he had a small package in his hand.

"I also went out to the pool house to get this," he said.

"What is it?" She felt like a kid.

"Something for you I wanted to give you privately. Here. Open it."

"I have one for you, too."

"Mine can wait."

With trembling fingers, Verity took the present. The box was heavy and she couldn't imagine what was inside. Untying the ribbon, she laid it on the counter, then pulled off the paper and did the same with that.

Curiously she lifted the white lid. "Oh, Leo. It's beautiful!" She removed from the box a crystal paperweight in the shape of a shooting star. Tears came to her eyes as she ran her fingers over it. "It's beautiful," she said again, all of her heartfelt emotion in her voice. "I can't believe you remembered."

"I remember everything you tell me," Leo murmured, taking her into his arms.

She had to tell him something he didn't know. "I saw a shooting star the night we rode on the beach."

"When?"

"On our way back. It was as if Sean approved . . . of us."

Leo tipped her chin up and sealed his lips to hers. It was a hungry kiss that told her they hadn't kissed for far too long. It was a possessive kiss, and she loved the idea that Leo wanted to make her his. It was a masterful kiss, relaying to her that he wanted to teach her everything he knew about two people coming together, joining their hearts and souls and minds.

When he broke away, they were both breathless. "If your dad weren't a guest in my house tonight, I'd carry you to my bedroom."

"You can still do that," she teased.

"Tonight's too risky. Heather could come in and ask when Santa's coming."

They both laughed.

He ran his thumb over her lips. "We have time, Verity. Plenty of time. Besides, enjoying the anticipation is half the fun." After another quick kiss on her lips, he said, "Go on to bed. I'm going to catch the

211

late news. I need something to distract myself from thinking about that kiss."

Still holding the box with the shooting star, she smiled at him. "Thank you for this. It means a lot."

"Good night, Verity. I hope you hear sleigh bells."

As she walked down the hall to her room, she knew she would. Tonight had been a perfect Christmas Eve. And tomorrow . . . if she and Leo had some time alone together, she'd tell him she loved him. Then maybe soon he could say those words, too.

She'd almost reached her room when she remembered the slice of pie they needed to leave out for Santa along with the glass of milk. She knew Heather would look for that empty glass and cleared plate. When she turned to go back into the great room, she heard music coming from a commercial on the TV. It sounded familiar.

ZING! It was the jingle for *ZING!*

She didn't intend to walk softly to the great room. She didn't really intend to spy on Leo as the commercial played on the big screen. But her gaze was riveted to him as she saw him stare at the images in fascination. He was watching her back as she walked away on the screen, the parasol over her shoulder.

Was that longing on his face?

Obviously, he hadn't recognized her. How could he? Only a glimpse of her face had shown for about half a second. And she looked so different in that commercial. She looked sophisticated and sexy and like everything a man could want in a woman.

With a flash of insight, she knew she could *be* that woman for Leo. If she could become that woman again, then maybe he could tell her he loved her.

When they went on their date, he was going to get the surprise of his life. She'd decided, after Matthew had bailed out of her life, she never wanted a man to be attracted to her again simply because of her physical appearance. She hadn't wanted a man who looked at the surface first, the inside later. But Leo had been attracted to her for what she was . . . for *who* she was. Now she wanted to show him she could be so much more. When they went on their date, he'd have a woman on his arm who would turn his head and keep it turned . . . toward her.

Chapter Ten

On the day of the concert, Verity stepped inside the doors of the exclusive dress shop with Jolene right behind her. "I pick up my contact lenses at three. Luckily the doctor had a cancellation and stocks the contacts I need. But he has a technician who explains how to wear them, how to clean them and all that, so that's why I'm going back this afternoon."

"When are you getting your hair done?"

"That's at four. Fortunately, the hairstylist could squeeze me in. So now, all I need is a dress. Are you sure women get dressed up for these concerts?"

"Absolutely," Jolene assured her with a wide grin. "They're an event in Avon Lake, especially around the holidays. You probably don't want anything sequined or beaded, but dressy is good. This store has great clothes as well as great sales after Christmas."

"Thanks for meeting me here. It's been so long since I bought a dress, I wanted another woman's perspective."

"I'll give you perspective. We'll find

something that will wow Leo. What are you going to do with your hair? Have it cut?"

"Not much. Just trimmed a little. I'm going to get one of those spiral perms."

"Leo's not going to even know you."

He was going to know her, all right. She was going to turn into his fantasy woman, the woman who'd mesmerized him on the TV screen.

The store's racks still had a lot of selections. Jolene bypassed the sportswear and everyday clothes to head straight for the party dresses. Verity flipped through the dresses, dismissing any that were beaded or sequined and one that was silver lamé.

"Too gaudy," Jolene offered with a shake of her head.

Verity agreed. Finally they selected three — a black velvet halter dress with a short straight skirt, high neck in front and a low vee that would bare her back. The second was a red, silky fabric with long sleeves and low décolletage. It had a straight skirt and a slit up the side. Finally, there was a white, wool dress with a sweetheart neckline, long sleeves and full skirt. Verity knew before she tried it on that it was simply too virginal. That wasn't the look she was going for. But

Jolene liked it, so she took it to the dressing room with them.

A half hour later, she left the store with Jolene, a wide grin on her face. "I knew I'd like that one best."

"I wish I could be there to see Leo's eyes pop out."

Verity laughed. "I didn't think I'd have an audience for the great 'reveal.' "

"I have a feeling it could be a night you'll never forget."

"I hope so," Verity decided fervently.

Jolene glanced at her watch. "We have time for lunch before you have to go to the ophthalmologist."

"Are you sure Tim won't mind watching the kids for another hour?"

"He won't mind. He takes days off over Christmas so he *can* spend time with them. There's a deli over on Bluebonnet. Why don't we stop in there? We could walk since the sun's shining today."

"I'm glad the rain stopped. My feet would get wet in those new shoes if I had to walk through puddles." The strappy, high-heeled sandals weren't like any shoes she'd ever bought before.

Suddenly Jolene grabbed her arm. "What about a coat? You can't wear a windbreaker with a dress like that." Jolene eyed Verity's jacket.

"Believe it or not, I have a cape I bought last year. It'll be perfect." She'd gotten it when she and Matthew had attended a dance at UT.

They stopped at Verity's car so she could put her packages inside.

"I got a call from Mom yesterday," Jolene disclosed.

"About anything important?"

"You could say that. She wanted to know why I thought Leo was interested in you."

Verity wasn't sure she wanted to hear this, but it was better to know what she was up against. "What did you say?"

"I told her he was interested because you're perfect for him."

"I bet that went over like a lead balloon."

"Actually, it didn't. She was very quiet for a while, but then she revealed that on Christmas Eve she realized Leo hadn't been as happy in his marriage as she'd thought he had. She also realized that since you came into his life, he's smiling again, and that was important. By the way, I think she liked your dad."

"I think he was fascinated by her and all the places she's been."

"I think she admired the fact that he raised you and your brother on his own."

Verity and Jolene started walking down the street. "Dad and I had a talk on Christmas Eve," Verity confided. "We connected in a way we never have before. When he left last night, I felt as if I'd found something that had been lost for a long time."

Jolene glanced over at her. "So this has been a particularly special holiday for you?"

"I hope it has been for Leo, too," she said softly.

"I think it has," Jolene assured her.

"When Dad comes to visit again, if your mom's in town, I'll ask her to come to dinner, too."

"Matchmaking?" Jolene asked with a raised brow.

"I wouldn't call it that," Verity answered with a smile.

The two women exchanged a look, and they both laughed.

When Heather didn't want to take a nap, she was a bundle of energy that just wouldn't quit. Thankful for the sunny day, Leo had taken her to a playground, then fed her lunch, hoping she'd be ready to rest for a while. But resting wasn't on her agenda.

"Hide-and-seek, Daddy," she said with

one of those smiles that made him feel like butter in her tiny hands.

"Okay, hide-and-seek. But only for a little while. Then you've got to rest. I don't want you cranky when you go see Joey and Randy tonight."

Jolene had offered to leave the boys with Tim, and she'd come babysit Heather. But he'd suggested Heather just stay overnight with her, instead. That way, he and Verity didn't have to worry about what time they got home. When they *did* get home, they wouldn't have to worry about being interrupted.

And just what might anyone interrupt? a little devil on Leo's shoulder asked.

Leo didn't have the answer to that. But he did know that tonight could be something special.

For the first round of hide-and-seek, Heather slipped behind the pink-and-white-striped chair in her bedroom, sure Leo wouldn't find her there. But he did, and she giggled when he tickled her.

Enthusiastically, she announced, "*Your* turn."

It didn't take Leo long to crouch down under the dining room table. After scurrying around the great room and calling "Daddy" a few times, she spotted him, ran toward him and gave him a giant hug.

"You're good at this," he told her with a laugh.

"I hide now," she said, and took off down the hall.

He knew where she was headed — to Verity's rooms.

Feeling like an intruder, he stepped inside Verity's sitting room and didn't see Heather at first glance. "Where are you?" he called.

After a quick look around, he pushed the bedroom door open wider, remembering how Heather had slipped under Verity's bed once before. He checked under there, but his daughter was nowhere to be found. Verity's closet didn't hold a little girl, either. Finally he knew what to do. Heather couldn't be quiet for more than a minute. He stood still and listened.

When he heard a rustling sound, he went into Verity's sitting room again. Then he saw the little feet peeking out under Verity's desk. When he went over there and pulled out the chair, Heather popped out, whirled around, and in her excitement brushed a few papers off of the desk.

As Heather ran out of the room and down the hall, Leo called after her, "I'm going to tickle you when I catch you."

He heard his daughter giggle.

Stooping, he picked up the papers that had fallen. One was a Christmas card that had opened, and in spite of himself, he read the writing inside. "You're a beautiful young woman who deserves love. Always, Will."

The Christmas card was a simple one with a Christmas tree on the front. There was no envelope with it.

Leo remembered the other letter Verity had received from Will. He remembered the man at the arts festival. He remembered Verity standing in the foyer of the Arts and Sciences Building in the shadows, a man close to her, his hand on her shoulder. Leo's gut turned, and all of it felt wrong.

Was Verity seeing this Will on her days off? Was she keeping secrets from him? Was she too young to understand monogamy and commitment?

That's what he'd been afraid of all along. Maybe she wasn't as inexperienced as he'd thought she was . . . or as she pretended to be. Was she really a virgin? Was *any* girl a virgin into her twenties these days?

Had he been an absolute fool?

The questions wouldn't stop swirling in his head. He had to confront Verity about it tonight before they went out. He had to know the truth.

He remembered Carolyn keeping a secret for three months, three months that had affected the rest of his life. If Verity was keeping secrets, he was going to find out what they were.

An hour later Leo had finally gotten Heather settled for her nap when the phone rang. Quickly snatching it up in the kitchen, he growled, "Montgomery here."

"You don't sound like a man who's going out on the town tonight," his sister jibed.

He didn't know if he was still going to be going out on the town tonight. He just knew that Verity had some explaining to do, and that was the first item on his agenda. "It took three stories to put Heather down for her nap. Somehow, I think her negotiation skills are better than mine. Did she learn them from you?"

Jolene laughed. "Could be." After a pause she said, "The reason I called is twofold. Verity said the two of you are grabbing leftovers to eat before you leave. You can give Heather a snack, but don't feed her supper. The boys want to order pizza after she arrives. And secondly, I'm going to come over and pick her up so you don't have to drop her off."

"I'm sure there's a reason you want to go out of your way."

"There is," Jolene admitted, with a lilt to her voice. "I want to see Verity before she leaves."

"Why?"

"Because I've been involved in the transformation process, and I want to see the result."

"Transformation?"

"You'll see. Anyway, the concert's at seven-thirty, right?"

"Right."

"I'll be there around six-thirty."

Since he wanted to confront Verity about what he'd seen in her sitting room, a talk would be easier after Jolene picked Heather up. "That sounds good. Thanks, Jolene."

After Jolene hung up, Leo went to the pool house for his briefcase. He would work at the kitchen table and stay occupied until he could have that talk with Verity.

When Verity came rushing into the house at 6:00, Leo heard her but didn't see her. Building a block tower with his daughter in the great room, he was aware of the front door opening.

Verity called, "Sorry I'm late. I've got to

get dressed. Are you and Heather okay?"

"Fine," he called. "Jolene's coming to pick her up, so you have time."

Seconds later he heard Verity's sitting room door open and close. He'd already changed into his suit. All they had to do was grab something to eat and they'd be on their way — after he asked her about that card and letter.

A half hour later Jolene rang the front doorbell and came in. "Anybody home?" she called brightly.

Leo had packed everything Heather would need in a small pink suitcase he'd bought his daughter for just that purpose. Now he set it next to the little table where Heather was coloring contentedly.

When Jolene stepped into the kitchen, she smiled at him. "Don't you look handsome. Mother would be proud."

He straightened the knot of his tie. "Thank goodness I don't have to wear one of these every day."

When Jolene laughed, he gave her a wry grin.

"Leo," Verity's soft voice came from the great room.

When he walked in there, he stopped abruptly, caught up by the vision of Verity Sumpter, who looked entirely like someone else. The black velvet dress draped over her figure, flattering every curve. Her hair was a mass of curls. Her eyes were so big —

He swore. He'd seen her looking like this before. In the ZING commercial!

"You look like the woman —"

"I am that woman," she admitted with a smile that he took as seductive.

Confusion and then anger burgeoned inside Leo. She'd been playing a role with him . . . playing him for a fool. "Why were you pretending to be somebody you weren't?" he demanded.

Her surprise at his tone showed. "I made that commercial over a year ago."

"That's not an answer. That doesn't explain why you kept a secret from me or why you've been hiding behind drab clothes and glasses." Suddenly everything about Verity seemed like a mirage — a mirage he'd needed to pull him out of his past. Yet, if it was a mirage, it wasn't real. *She* might not be real. If she'd been deceptive about who she was, then she might be deceptive about other things.

"I don't know why you're playing at being a nanny or why you've hidden who you really are, but it makes me wonder what else you've been hiding. Are you seeing someone behind my back?"

Her brown eyes, which looked so impossibly large without her glasses, widened with surprise. "I have no idea what you're talking about. I haven't been seeing anyone."

He realized now that her innocent act could be just that . . . an act. He motioned angrily toward Verity's sitting room. "Heather and I were playing hide-and-seek this afternoon. She hid under your desk. When I found her, she accidently knocked down some papers. One of them was a Christmas card from Will. It sounded to me as if you two have something going on."

Verity had paled at Leo's accusations, but now spots of color again dotted her cheeks, making the blush she'd applied seem even rosier.

He heard his sister murmur, "Leo . . ." in a warning tone. But he didn't pay any attention to her until she gathered Heather into her arms and said to her, "We're going to play in your room for a few minutes," then carried her away.

Verity's gaze hadn't moved from Leo's. "Your question sounds more like an accusation," she said, her voice trembling. "Do you really believe I'd see someone behind your back?"

"If you would hide what you really look like all these weeks —"

"Hide what I look like?" She brushed her new curls behind one ear. "Let me tell you who I am, Leo, because you don't seem to know me. I grew up as a tomboy because I loved being with Sean and I wanted to earn my dad's approval. I never cared about dresses and designer jeans or having my ears pierced. Then I went to college, and still poured my attention into sports and studies, until one day a casting agent approached me. A new soda was going to hit the market, and the company wanted to use college-age girls and guys, to target that audience. I wasn't interested, but Sean thought it would be a blast. So, I agreed to do it. Professionals trained me how to walk and smile. A stylist curled my hair. A makeup artist applied makeup."

Suddenly she held out her arms and pirouetted. "This was born. Did I like the new image? I wasn't sure it fit. But I had the contact lenses, and the curls would take a while to grow out. Matthew was attracted to the new look, and we started dating. That should have taught me something, but I guess I'm not a fast learner."

Leo still wasn't ready to believe her and

needed further explanations. "Why did you go back to wearing oversize sweatshirts? And glasses?"

"Because after Sean died, I just didn't care anymore. I kept getting my hair trimmed and eventually the perm relaxed, the red highlights washed out. Then I took this job with you, and I began caring about everything again. I came back to life. Heather filled my heart with joy. You filled it with —" She paused, then went on. "I just thought you'd like this version of me, that if I wowed you, you might be able to admit your feelings."

"What about the card?" he asked hoarsely, still unable to let that go.

"That card is from my advisor, Dr. Will Stratford. By the way, he's old enough to be my grandfather. He was easy to confide in, and I told him I was . . . falling in love with you. But my feelings don't seem to mean very much. If you think I would see a man behind your back, then you don't know me at all, no matter what I'm wearing."

With that declaration, Verity turned and practically ran down the hall to her room.

Leo heard the slam of her door. Feeling shellshocked, he sank down onto the sofa. That's where Jolene found him a few minutes later. He looked up. "Where's Heather?"

"She's changing the clothes on her doll. What happened here?"

"You tell me." He yanked on the knot of his tie and opened it.

"In a nutshell, you blew it," Jolene concluded.

Finally he stared at his sister. "Did you know about the commercial?"

With a shake of her head, Jolene sat on the sofa beside him. "No. Verity didn't tell me. It wasn't long after she started working for you that I thought she looked familiar. That must have been when the ZING commercial started playing. But now that I think about it, you don't actually see her face on the screen for more than a split second. And all that hair. She looked so different."

"Why did she decide to make the transformation tonight?"

"Lots of reasons, I imagine. But I suspect the main one is because she wanted you to fall head over heels for her. She wanted to wow you and give you that sucker punch that would bring you to your knees and make you admit you loved her."

Verity had sucker punched him all right, but the blow had nothing to do with the way she looked. When she explained why she'd transformed herself again, he'd realized what a terrible mistake he'd made. He'd realized his doubts had ruined everything between them.

"She's probably packing," he muttered.

"Is there a good reason she *shouldn't* be packing?"

"Hell, yes! I need her in my life. Heather needs her. She's the best thing that's ever happened to us. And I —"

"Say it, Leo," Jolene prompted. "If you don't acknowledge it, and you don't say it, you're going to lose her."

Taking a deep breath, he admitted, "I love her."

The silence in the house was deafening.

Jolene glanced over her shoulder and down the hall to the bedrooms. "I'd better check on Heather."

Now that he'd admitted his feelings for Verity, he knew he had to do something about them . . . something concrete. "Can you stay here for a little while? I have to run an errand."

"Now?"

"Yes, now. Don't let Verity leave."

"What am I supposed to do, chain her to a chair?"

"I'm serious, Jolene. Don't let her leave. Make up some excuse. You have to keep her here until I get back."

"All right. I'll try. But if she wants to drive away, Leo, you know there's really nothing I can do to stop her."

He swore at the thought and the mess he'd made of everything. "I know. If she does leave, just make sure you find out where she's going . . . because I intend to go after her."

When Leo returned from his trip to the jewelry store, Jolene informed him Verity hadn't come out of her room. She hadn't tried to talk to her because she knew that was *his* job.

Gathering up Heather and her small suitcase, Jolene went to the door where Leo gave Heather a hug and a kiss. His daughter waved happily at him as Jolene carried her to her car.

Removing a tiny box from the jewelry store bag, Leo went to Verity's room and knocked. When she didn't answer, he knocked again. "Verity. Open the door."

After a few endless moments she did. He saw the tear tracks on her cheeks, and his chest felt tight. He'd never meant to hurt her. He'd never meant to doubt her.

She didn't say anything, just moved aside to let him enter. But he wasn't going to let her keep distance between them.

Taking her hand, he pulled her to the sofa and sat beside her. "I was afraid you'd pack your bags and go."

She stared straight ahead, rather than at him. "I thought about it, but I couldn't leave. . . ." Then she looked at him, and he saw everything that she was feeling in her eyes.

"I hope that means what I think it means," he said huskily.

He'd been holding the small velvet box in his hands. Now he opened his fingers and showed it to her.

Verity's gaze went from the box to him.

"I've been an absolute fool. I *have* used every excuse in the book to keep from falling in love with you. But I *am* in love with you. Why else do you think I went so crazy when I saw that Christmas card?"

"You were jealous?" she asked a bit incredulously.

"Of course I was jealous! You are a beautiful, intelligent, talented woman, Verity." He brushed the curls from the side of her face. "Whether you have your hair curled, you're wearing glasses or you're dressed in jeans and playing with Heather, I fell in love with *you,* not a fantasy woman."

He opened the black velvet box. "Will you accept this ring? Will you marry me?"

Her mouth opened. Her voice was thready as she said in amazement, "I can't believe you're asking. I can't believe you want me to be your wife." She stared down at the princess cut diamond as if she couldn't believe her eyes.

Sliding the ring from the box, he held it out to her. "Will you let me put this on your finger?"

Trembling, she gave him her hand, and he slipped the diamond on her ring finger.

When she looked up at him, tears were brimming in her eyes. "Yes, I'll marry you, Leo. I love you."

Leo didn't realize he'd been holding his breath. Verity's answer meant the world to him. When his arms went around her, she lifted her face to his. When he kissed her, he let down all his walls, and his fervor told her exactly what he was feeling.

Breaking the kiss, but not leaning too far away, he asked, "When will you marry me?"

She was smiling now, and her eyes sparkled with her happiness. "Whenever you'd like."

"Soon," he breathed. "I don't know how long I can wait to make you mine."

"We don't have to wait," she assured him.

Holding her face between his palms, he kissed her again. Afterward he said, "Yes, we do. You told me once, you were saving yourself for the right man. I want to prove to you I *am* the right man. Our wedding night will be special for both of us."

Then he took his bride-to-be in his arms, grateful for all the love she'd brought into his life, grateful for the chance to share a future with her. He loved Verity Sumpter, and he would prove it to her for the rest of their lives.

Epilogue

On the evening of January fifth, the Twelfth Night — the last day of the Christmas season, Verity walked down the aisle of the college chapel, candlelight flickering on the white runner that showed her the path to her groom. Her father's arm steadied her. Her satiny, princess-style wedding gown billowed about her as her veil flowed in front of her face. The chapel was still beautifully decorated with poinsettias, but she hardly noticed anything except for the man she was going to marry. Jolene had walked down the aisle first in a green velvet dress, followed by little Heather in matching green velvet with a basket of yellow rose petals. Verity's heart was so full she could hardly breathe. As she approached Leo, it beat even faster.

Once she and her father reached the altar, her dad lifted her veil and kissed her cheek. "Be happy," he said so fervently, she knew if she was happy, *he* would be, too. Then he placed her hand in Leo's, and she stood before the minister with her soon-to-be husband.

Always handsome, Leo was over the top

tonight in his black tuxedo. He was looking at her as if he couldn't bear to turn away. She felt the same, and tears came to her eyes.

He squeezed her hand and said in a low, husky voice, "I love you."

"I love you, too."

The minister, a man with tortoiseshell glasses and gray hair, smiled benignly. "I think you two could do this without me. But just to make it official . . ."

The minister began the service.

As Verity promised to love, honor and cherish Leo, her heart overflowed with happiness. As Leo promised to love, honor and cherish Verity, she heard the deep sincerity in his vows, and knew they'd love each other for a lifetime . . . and more.

After the minister gave his blessing, Leo kissed her soundly with a yearning she was feeling, too . . . a yearning they would satisfy tonight.

They turned as husband and wife to greet their guests, and Verity spotted friends who had traveled from Galveston, spotted Jolene and Tim, Leo's mother and Dr. Will Stratford. The professor winked at her and she smiled. She barely noticed the photographer who'd captured every wonderful moment of the ceremony. Soon he would join them on a ship Leo had rented for the evening where they and their guests would enjoy the wedding reception.

Heather came running toward them then, and Leo scooped her up. The three of them walked to the back of the church together, a family at last.

The limo waited for them outside. They were stopping at the beach first where they could stargaze for a short while and breathe in the magnitude of the life they would share together.

Descending the church steps, Verity could see the night was filled with stars and promise. As Leo's arm held her close, Heather pointed up to the sky. "Look."

Verity and Leo saw it at the same moment — a shooting star, streaking across the heavens in an arc above them.

As moved as Verity, Leo said in a gravelly voice, "I think that's your twin's seal of approval."

Verity blew a kiss into the heavens and then raised her face to Leo's. His kiss was a mixture of gentle and sweet and possessive.

Together they climbed into the limo with Heather who Verity already loved as her own. Together they would make a life. Together they would form a family.

A car seat was waiting in the limo for Heather. Leo buckled her in and sat across from her with his arm around Verity.

"Are you ready for this new adventure, Mrs. Montgomery?" he asked with a wide grin.

"I'm ready for any adventure . . . as long as we live it together," Verity replied.

Leo held her close as the chauffeur drove them away . . . into their happily-ever-after.

About the Author

Karen Rose Smith, award-winning author of over fifty published novels, enjoyed Shakespeare's works when she studied them in college. As an English teacher, she particularly liked sharing them with her ninth and tenth graders, encouraging appreciation for the Bard's plot lines, language and grasp of universal emotions. Then she never suspected crafting emotional and romantic stories would become *her* life's work! Married for thirty-four years, she and her husband reside in Pennsylvania with their two cats, Ebbie and London. Readers can e-mail Karen through her Web site at www.karenrosesmith.com or write to her at P.O. Box 1545, Hanover, PA 17331.

The employees of Thorndike Press hope you have enjoyed this Large Print book. All our Thorndike and Wheeler Large Print titles are designed for easy reading, and all our books are made to last. Other Thorndike Press Large Print books are available at your library, through selected bookstores, or directly from us.

For information about titles, please call:

(800) 223-1244

or visit our Web site at:

www.gale.com/thorndike
www.gale.com/wheeler

To share your comments, please write:

Publisher
Thorndike Press
295 Kennedy Memorial Drive
Waterville, ME   04901